I

THE BAND PLAYS

THE BAND PLAYS

The Boys in the Band
The Men From the Boys

alyson books
los angeles

MANUFACTURED IN THE UNITED STATES OF AMERICA.

THIS TRADE PAPERBACK ORIGINAL IS PUBLISHED BY ALYSON PUBLICATIONS,
P.O. BOX 4371, LOS ANGELES, CALIFORNIA 90078-4371.

THE BOYS IN THE BAND FIRST PUBLISHED BY FARRAR, STRAUS & GIROUX: 1968

FIRST ALYSON EDITION: SEPTEMBER 2003

03 04 05 06 07 a 10 9 8 7 6 5 4 3 2 1

ISBN 1-55583-831-6

LIBRARY OF CONGRESS CATALOGING-IN-PUBLICATION DATA
    CROWLEY, MART, 1935–
        THE BAND PLAYS : THE BOYS IN THE BAND AND ITS SEQUEL THE MEN FROM THE
    BOYS / MART CROWLEY.—1ST ED.
        ISBN 1-55583-831-6 (PBK.)
        1. GAY MEN—DRAMA. I. CROWLEY, MART, 1935– BOYS IN THE BAND. II. CROWLEY,
    MART, 1935– MEN FROM BOYS. III. TITLE: BOYS IN THE BAND. IV. TITLE: MEN FROM
    BOYS. V. TITLE.
    PS3553.R6B36 2003
    812'.54—DC21   2003052084

CREDITS
•"HAPPY BIRTHDAY" © 1935 BY SUMMY-BIRCHARD COMPANY, EVANSTON, ILLINOIS.
  COPYRIGHT RENEWED. ALL RIGHTS RESERVED. USED BY PERMISSION IN THE BOYS
  IN THE BAND.
•"GET HAPPY" © 1929 BY REMICK MUSIC CORPORATION. REPRINTED BY PERMISSION
  OF WARNER BROS.–SEVEN ARTS MUSIC IN THE BOYS IN THE BAND.
•"QUE RESTE-T-IL DE NOS AMOURS?" © 1946, 1955, 1956 BY EDITIONS SALABERT,
  UNIVERSAL MCA MUSIC PUBLISHING (CANADA-USA) (IN THE MEN FROM THE BOYS).
•"I'M NOT THE MAN I PLANNED" © 2003 BY LARRY GROSSMAN (MUSIC) AND MART
  CROWLEY (LYRICS) (IN THE MEN FROM THE BOYS).
•COVER ART BY HILARY KNIGHT.
•COVER DESIGN BY MATT SAMS.

THIS COLLECTION IS FOR

MITCH DOUGLAS

Contents

Foreword

A good play closely resembles life—"with the dull parts cut out," as someone once said. Just so, a good play not only withstands the test of time, it also addresses one or more central and common elements in human experience. By these and perhaps any other critical standards, Mart Crowley's comic drama *The Boys in the Band* (1968) is a very good play, and a classic one too. *The Men From the Boys* (2002) is, I dare to predict, destined for similar eminence.

In the post-Stonewall era, reading *The Boys in the Band,* or attending a first-rate production of it, one is struck by the sheer gallantry of the playwright's wit—and by the ferocity of his rage against the toll exacted by ignorance and prejudice. Very much in the tradition of Richard Brinsley Sheridan and Oscar Wilde, Crowley discloses—with agile humor and a breathtaking kind of spiritual integrity—the wounds inflicted by social and cultural bigotry, as we see them refracted in the souls of nine young men gathered for a birthday party. These chaps are sometimes flamboyant and often frightened, to be sure, but that is what makes them and their histories, viewpoints, issues, dilemmas, and desires so recognizable and comprehensible. That they also elicit our unsentimental sympathy is a credit to the playwright's deepest skills and overarching humanity.

Carefully observing all the classical unities, *The Boys in the Band* is wrenchingly cathartic. At the final curtain, after what amounts to a painful evening of something like a modern auto-da-fé, each character has a renewed hope as well as a deeper connection to someone. Larry and his mate Hank reach across their misunderstandings toward a new patience with each other. Bernard and Emory, more deeply disenfranchised by the accident of race and personality than the others, limp away as supportive friends, tending each other's physical and emotional bruises. Alan, certainly in crisis over his marriage, returns to his wife—but not, it seems, to anything like marital bliss. Harold, whose laser insight cannot alleviate his own psychic pain, brutally diagnoses the source of Michael's habitual self-torture—but still promises the long arm of ongoing friendship.

Crowley's most moving scene, however—and that in which he reveals his essential compassion for all these men and their antitypes—is saved for the finale, in which he recapitulates and renews the bond between the self-loathing Michael and his loyal friend Donald. But no life is destroyed during this dark night of the spirit; to the contrary, each is illuminated, and there is the distinct impression that healing is possible—perhaps even likely.

The Boys in the Band had been playing to capacity crowds for more than a year when a crowd of gay men failed to yield to a platoon of surly, homophobic policemen at the Stonewall Inn in New York's Greenwich Village on June 28, 1969. Almost right up until that now-mythic date, it was somewhat unimaginable for a play to present homosexuals who struggled with the accumulated hatred of generations of prejudice and its effect on their own benighted spirits; more to the point, it was unthinkable that they would not commit suicide or murder or die of some addiction or be killed before the final curtain.

Of course, *Boys* is a play of its time—what work of art is not? So is Lorraine Hansberry's classic *A Raisin in the Sun*, which deals with what is now called low self-esteem among American black people. One might add, so is *Hamlet*, about low self-esteem in the heart of a confused young Danish prince who doesn't much like his family.

But isn't it important to know where we've come from? In this regard, *Boys* is a cautionary tale. There was, after all, a time when society tacitly endorsed the dreadful lie that minorities like gays and blacks ought to be full of self-loathing: "If only we could just learn not to hate ourselves so very much," as Michael says. It would take years—for the character and his society—to discover the deepest sources of this unnecessary suffering. Battles have been won, but skirmishes still erupt all the time, everywhere.

§   §   §

I had the good fortune to see the original New York cast of *The Boys in the Band* in 1968. In the autumn of 2002, I was in the San Francisco audience for the premiere of *The Men From the Boys*, one of the few successful sequel plays in American theater history. "Before there were marches, there was a band," says Emory, now sixty-two, campy and valiant as ever. He and the boys once led that band; as men, they still do, but now the music is muted. Except for Cowboy, Alan, and Larry, all the original characters are here—in important ways, they've been chastened by time and age, by chance and choice. They don't seem to have quite the cunning and guile of their youth, and the earlier edge of contempt that flashed so blithely has been mercifully softened. But there is still the healthy reaction against cant and an awareness that cruelty gets you nowhere. The men haven't become wisdom figures or exemplars for younger gays: Crowley is too savvy about human nature for that, and besides, young men of any description rarely want exemplars. One of them, however, is alert enough to recognize the significance of enduring camaraderie among the elders: "How could anybody's younger friends stand up next to you guys...for longevity of friendship?" In a crucial way, of course, friendship is at the emotional core of both plays.

Among Crowley's remarkable achievements in *Men* is a kind of Chekhovian wistfulness, represented by the motif of life's fundamental fragility. *Boys* was set at a birthday party; it's a bold stroke to set *Men* at a "celebration of life" for one of them, recently deceased (not, let us note, from AIDS). The clan gathers, six old friends and three arrivistes. Of course, there's an undertaste of melancholy beneath the awkward festivity—but what raw courage has attended the maturation of these older men, now leaning from both sides against the fulcrum of age sixty! "Getting old is the greatest sin in America," observes Harold, his sharpness unblunted by the years. For the most part, the men who were once boys seem to have accepted aging with admirable grace, not just steely stoicism. They sin boldly, in fact, by reveling in the prerogatives of age.

Michael, for example, speaks not only for himself when he tells young Scott, "I don't know how I survived...I met people who were smarter and wiser than I was, and I learned from them. Like I've tried to pass on things to you. Like believing in yourself. Your *self*: that thing you feel when you go through a revolving door—that post, that center, that something *unshakable*...around which everything else spins!"

At the end, there is the certainty of fresh challenge and inevitable heartbreak—realities that will, however, be leavened by the kind of deep solidarity that only true friendship effects. "Callyatomorrow!" was Harold's final exit line to Michael in *Boys*—just as it is in *Men*, and just as it will be as they face a future of darkness, diminishment, and the sort of devotion that has nothing to do with eros.

"There's something very poignant," says a character in another play by Mart Crowley, "about the frailty of a group of vulnerable human beings, struggling valiantly." That is a fair summary of the playwright's wise, witty, grave, and astonishingly affirmative vision of human possibility in all his works, and perhaps nowhere more acutely than in this bright and brilliant duet.

—DONALD SPOTO

THE BOYS IN THE BAND

FOR

HOWARD JEFFREY

AND

DOUGLAS MURRAY

§   §   §

The Boys in the Band was first performed in January 1968 at the Playwrights Unit, Vandam Theatre, Charles Gnys, managing director.

The Boys in the Band was first produced on the New York stage by Richard Barr and Charles Woodward Jr. at Theatre Four on April 14, 1968. The play was designed by Peter Harvey and directed by Robert Moore.

The original cast was:

MICHAEL	*Kenneth Nelson*
DONALD	*Frederick Combs*
EMORY	*Cliff Gorman*
LARRY	*Keith Prentice*
HANK	*Laurence Luckinbill*
BERNARD	*Reuben Greene*
COWBOY	*Robert La Tourneaux*
HAROLD	*Leonard Frey*
ALAN	*Peter White*

The play is divided into two acts. The action is continuous and occurs one evening within the time necessary to perform the script.

Characters:

MICHAEL	Thirty, average face, smartly groomed
DONALD	Twenty-eight, medium-blond, wholesome American good looks
EMORY	Thirty-three, small, frail, very plain
LARRY	Twenty-nine, extremely handsome
HANK	Thirty-two, tall, solid, athletic, attractive
BERNARD	Twenty-eight, Negro, nice-looking
COWBOY	Twenty-two, light-blond, muscle-bound, too pretty
HAROLD	Thirty-two, dark, lean, strong limbs, unusual Semitic face
ALAN	Thirty, aristocratic, Anglo-Saxon features

A c t   1

A smartly appointed duplex apartment in the East Fifties, New York,
consisting of a living room and, on a higher level, a bedroom. Bossa
nova music blasts from a phonograph.

MICHAEL, wearing a robe, enters from the kitchen, carrying some
liquor bottles. He crosses to set them on a bar, looks to see if the
room is in order, moves toward the stairs to the bedroom level,
doing a few improvised dance steps en route. In the bedroom, he
crosses before a mirror, studies his hair—sighs. He picks up comb
and a hair dryer, goes to work.

The downstairs front door buzzer sounds. A beat. MICHAEL stops,
listens, turns off the dryer. More buzzing. MICHAEL quickly goes to
the living room, turns off the music, opens the door to reveal DON-
ALD, dressed in khakis and a Lacoste shirt, carrying an airline zip-
per bag.

MICHAEL
Donald! You're about a day and a half early!

DONALD
[Enters]
The doctor canceled!

MICHAEL
Canceled! How'd you get inside?

DONALD
The street door was open.

MICHAEL
You wanna drink?

DONALD
[Going to bedroom to deposit his bag]
Not until I've had my shower. I want something to work out
today—I want to try to relax and enjoy something.

MICHAEL
You in a blue funk because of the doctor?

DONALD
[*Returning*]
Christ, no. I was depressed long before I got *there*.

MICHAEL
Why'd the prick cancel?

DONALD
A virus or something. He looked awful.

MICHAEL
[*Holding up a shopping bag*]
Well, this'll pick you up. I went shopping today and bought all
kinds of goodies. Sandalwood soap…

DONALD
[*Removing his socks and shoes*]
I feel better already.

MICHAEL
[*Producing articles*]
…Your very own toothbrush because I'm sick to death of your using
mine.

DONALD
How do you think *I* feel.

MICHAEL
You've had worse things in your mouth.
[*Holds up a cylindrical can*]
And, also for you…something called "Control." Notice nowhere is it
called hair spray—just simply "Control." And the words "For Men"
are written about thirty-seven times all over the goddamn can!

DONALD
It's called Butch Assurance.

MICHAEL
Well, it's *still* hair spray—no matter if they call it *"Balls"*!
[*DONALD laughs*]
It's all going on your very own shelf, which is to be labeled: Donald's
Saturday Night Douche Kit. By the way, are you spending the night?

DONALD
Nope. I'm driving back. I still get very itchy when I'm in this town
too long. I'm not that well yet.

6

MICHAEL
That's what you say every weekend.

DONALD
Maybe after about ten more years of analysis I'll be able to stay one
night.

MICHAEL
Maybe after about ten more years of analysis you'll be able to move
back to town permanently.

DONALD
If I live that long.

MICHAEL
You will. If you don't kill yourself on the Long Island Expressway
some early Sunday morning. I'll never know how you can tank up
on martinis and make it back to the Hamptons in one piece.

DONALD
Believe me, it's easier than getting here. Ever had an anxiety attack
at sixty miles an hour? Well, tonight I was beside myself to get to
the doctor—and just as I finally make it, rush in, throw myself on
the couch, and vomit out how depressed I am, he says, "Donald, I
have to cancel tonight—I'm just too sick."

MICHAEL
Why didn't you tell him you're sicker than he is.

DONALD
He already knows *that*.
        [*DONALD goes to the bedroom, drops his shoes and socks.* MICHAEL
        follows]

MICHAEL
Why didn't the prick call you and cancel. Suppose you'd driven all
this way for nothing.

DONALD
        [*Removing his shirt*]
Why do you keep calling him a prick?

MICHAEL
Whoever heard of an analyst having a session with a patient for two
hours on Saturday evening.

7

DONALD
He simply prefers to take Mondays off.

MICHAEL
Works late on Saturday and takes Monday off—what is he, a psychi-
atrist or a hairdresser?

DONALD
Actually, he's both. He shrinks my head and combs me out.
    [*Lies on the bed*]
Besides, I had to come in town to a birthday party anyway. Right?

MICHAEL
You had to remind me. If there's one thing I'm not ready for, it's
five screaming queens singing "Happy Birthday."

DONALD
Who's coming?

MICHAEL
They're really all Harold's friends. It's *his* birthday and I want
everything to be just the way he'd want it. I don't want to have to
listen to him kvetch about how nobody ever does anything for anybody but themselves.

DONALD
Himself.

MICHAEL
Himself. I think you know everybody anyway—they're the same
old tired fairies you've seen around since the day one. Actually,
there'll be seven, counting Harold and you and me.

DONALD
Are you calling me a screaming queen or a tired fairy?

MICHAEL
Oh, I beg your pardon—six tired screaming fairy queens and one
anxious queer.

DONALD
You don't think Harold'll mind my being here, do you? Technically,
I'm *your* friend, not his.

8

MICHAEL
If she doesn't like it, she can twirl on it. Listen, I'll be out of your way in just a second. I've only got one more thing to do.

DONALD
Surgery, so early in the evening?

MICHAEL
Çunt! That's French, with a cedilla.
		[*Gives him a crooked third finger, goes to mirror*]
I've just got to comb my hair for the thirty-seventh time. Hair—that's singular. My hair, without exaggeration, is clearly falling on the floor. And *fast*, baby!

DONALD
You're totally paranoid. You've got plenty of hair.

MICHAEL
What you see before you is a masterpiece of deception. My hairline starts about here.
		[*Indicates his crown*]
All this is just tortured forward.

DONALD
Well, I hope, for your sake, no strong wind comes up.

MICHAEL
If one does, I'll be in terrible trouble. I will then have a bald head and shoulder-length fringe.
		[*Runs his fingers through his hair, holds it away from his scalp, dips the top of his head so that* DONALD *can see.* DONALD *is silent*]
Not good, huh?

DONALD
Not the best.

MICHAEL
It's called, "getting old." Ah, life is such a grand design—spring, summer, fall, winter, death. Who*ever* could have thought it up?

DONALD
No one *we* know, that's for sure.

MICHAEL
[*Turns to study himself in the mirror, sighs*]
Well, one thing you can say for masturbation...you certainly
don't have to look your best.
[*Slips out of the robe, flings it at* DONALD. DONALD *laughs, takes the robe,
exits to the bath.* MICHAEL *takes a sweater out of a chest, pulls it on*]

MICHAEL
What are you so depressed about? I mean, other than the usual
everything.
[*A beat*]

DONALD
[*Reluctantly*]
I really don't want to get into it.

MICHAEL
Well, if you're not going to tell me, how can we have a conversation
in depth—a warm, rewarding, meaningful friendship?

DONALD
Up yours!

MICHAEL
[*Southern accent*]
Why, Cap'n Butler, how you talk!
[*Pause.* DONALD *appears in the doorway holding a glass of water
and a small bottle of pills.* MICHAEL *looks up*]

DONALD
It's just that today I finally realized that I was *raised* to be a failure. I
was *groomed* for it.
[*A beat*]

MICHAEL
You know, there was a time when you could have said that to me
and I wouldn't have known what the hell you were talking about.

DONALD
[*Takes some pills*]
Naturally, it all goes back to Evelyn and Walt.

MICHAEL

Naturally. When doesn't it go back to Mom and Pop? Unfortunately, we all had an Evelyn and a Walt. The crumbs! Don't you love that word—crumb? Oh, I love it! It's a real Barbara Stanwyck word.
   [*A la Stanwyck's frozen-lipped Brooklyn accent*]
"Cau'll me a keab, you kr-rumm."

DONALD

Well, I see all vestiges of sanity for this evening are now officially shot to hell.

MICHAEL

Oh, Donald, you're so serious tonight! You're fun-starved, baby, and I'm eating for two!

   [*Sings*]
"Forget your troubles, c'mon, get happy! You better chase all your blues away. Shout Hallelujah! C'mon get happy…"
   [*Sees DONALD isn't buying it*]
—what's more boring than a queen doing a Judy Garland imitation?

DONALD

A queen doing a Bette Davis imitation.

MICHAEL

Meanwhile—back at the Evelyn and Walt Syndrome.

DONALD

America's Square Peg and America's Round Hole.

MICHAEL

Christ, how sick analysts must get of hearing how mommy and daddy made their darlin' into a fairy.

DONALD

It's beyond just that now. Today I finally began to see how some of the other pieces of the puzzle relate to them.— Like why I never finished anything I started in my life…my neurotic compulsion to not succeed. I've realized it was always when I failed that Evelyn loved me the most—because it displeased Walt, who wanted perfection. And when I fell short of the mark she was only too happy to make up for it with her love. So I began to identify failing with winning my mother's love. And I began to fail on purpose to get it. I didn't finish Cornell—I couldn't keep a job in this town. I simply retreated to a room over a garage and scrubbing floors in order to keep alive. Failure is the only thing with which I feel at home. Because it is what I was taught at home.

MICHAEL
Killer whales is what they are. Killer whales. How many whales
could a killer whale kill...

DONALD
A lot, especially if they get them when they were babies.
[*Pause.* MICHAEL *suddenly tears off his sweater, throws it in the air,
letting it land where it may, whips out another, pulls it on as he
starts down the stairs for the living room.* DONALD *follows*]
Hey! Where're you going?

MICHAEL
To make drinks! I think we need about thirty-seven!

DONALD
Where'd you get *that* sweater?

MICHAEL
This clever little shop on the right bank called Hermès.

DONALD
I work my ass off for forty-five lousy dollars a week *scrubbing* floors
and you waltz around throwing cashmere sweaters on them.

MICHAEL
The one on the floor in the bedroom is vicuña.

DONALD
I *beg* your pardon.

MICHAEL
You could get a job doing something else. Nobody holds a gun to
your head to be a charwoman. That is, how you say, your neurosis.

DONALD
Gee, and I thought it's why I was born.

MICHAEL
Besides, just because I *wear* expensive clothes doesn't necessarily
mean they're paid for.

DONALD
That is, how you say, *your* neurosis.

MICHAEL
I'm a spoiled brat, so what do I know about being mature. The
only thing mature means to me is *Victor* Mature, who was in all
those pictures with Betty Grable.
        [*Sings à la Grable*]
"I can't begin to tell you, how much you mean to me..."
Betty sang that in 1945. '45?— '43. No, '43 was *Coney Island*, which
was remade in '50 as *Wabash Avenue*. Yes, *Dolly Sisters* was in '45.

DONALD
How did I manage to miss these momentous events in the American
cinema? I can understand people having an affinity for the stage—but
movies are such garbage, who can take them seriously?

MICHAEL
Well, I'm sorry if your sense of art is offended. Odd as it may seem,
there wasn't any Shubert Theatre in Hot Coffee, Mississippi!

DONALD
However—thanks to the silver screen, your neurosis has got style. It
takes a certain flair to squander one's unemployment check at
Pavillion.

MICHAEL
What's so snappy about being head over heels in debt. The only
thing smart about it is the ingenious ways I dodge the bill collec-
tors.

DONALD
Yeah. Come to think of it, you're the type that gives faggots a bad
name.

MICHAEL
And you, Donald, *you* are a credit to the homosexual. A reliable,
hardworking, floor-scrubbing, bill-paying fag who don't owe nothin'
to nobody.

DONALD
I am a model fairy.
        [*MICHAEL has taken some ribbon and paper and begun to wrap
        HAROLD's birthday gift*]

MICHAEL

You think it's just nifty how I've always flitted from Beverly Hills to Rome to Acapulco to Amsterdam, picking up a lot of one-night stands and a lot of custom-made duds along the trail, but I'm here to tell you that the only place in all those miles—the only place I've ever been *happy*—was on the goddamn plane.

[*Puffs up the bow on the package, continues*]

Bored with Scandinavia, try Greece. Fed up with dark meat, try light. Hate tequila, what about Slivovitz? Tired of boys, what about girls—or how about boys and girls mixed and in what combination? And if you're sick of people, what about poppers? Or pot or pills or the hard stuff. And can you think of anything else the bad baby would like to indulge his spoiled-rotten, stupid, empty, boring, self-ish, self-centered self in? Is that what you think has style, Donald? Huh? Is that what you think you've missed out on—my hysterical escapes from country to country, party to party, bar to bar, bed to bed, hangover to hangover, and all of it, hand to mouth!

[*A beat*]

Run, charge, run, buy, borrow, make, spend, run, squander, beg, run, run, run, waste, waste, *waste!*

[*A beat*]

And why? And why?

DONALD

Why, Michael? Why?

MICHAEL

I really don't want to get into it.

DONALD

Then how can we have a conversation in depth?

MICHAEL

Oh, you know it all by heart anyway. Same song, second verse. Because my Evelyn refused to let me grow up. She was determined to keep me a child forever and she did one helluva job of it. And my Walt stood by and let her do it.

[*A beat*]

What you see before you is a thirty-year-old infant. And it was all done in the name of love—what *she* labeled love and probably sin-cerely believed to be love, when what she was really doing was feeding her own need—satisfying her own loneliness.

[*A beat*]

She made me into a girlfriend dash lover.

[*A beat*]

14

We went to all those goddamn cornball movies together. I picked out her clothes for her and told her what to wear and she'd take me to the beauty parlor with her and we'd both get our hair bleached and a permanent and a manicure.

[*A beat*]

And Walt let this happen.

[*A beat*]

And she convinced me that I was a sickly child who couldn't run and play and sweat and get knocked around—oh, no! I was frail and pale and, to hear her tell it, practically female. I can't tell you the thousands of times she said to me, "I declare, Michael, you should have been a girl." And I guess I should have—I was frail and pale and bleached and curled and bedded down with hot-water bottles and my dolls and my paper dolls, and my doll clothes and my dollhouses!

[*Quick beat*]

And Walt bought them for me!

[*Beat. With increasing speed*]

And she nursed me and put Vicks salve on my chest and cold cream on my face and told me what beautiful eyes I had and what pretty lips I had. She bathed me in the same tub with her until I grew too big for the two of us to fit. She made me sleep in the same bed with her until I was fourteen years old—until I finally flatly refused to spend one more night there. She didn't want to prepare me for life or how to be out in the world on my own, or I might have left her. But I left anyway. This goddamn cripple finally wrenched free and limped away. And here I am—unequipped, undisciplined, untrained, unprepared, and unable to live!

[*A beat*]

And do you know until this day she still says, "I don't care if you're seventy years old, you'll always be my baby." And can I tell you how that drives me mad! Will that bitch never understand that what I'll always *be* is her son—but that I haven't been her baby for twenty-five years!

[*A beat*]

And don't get me wrong. I know it's easy to cop out and blame Evelyn and Walt and say it was *their* fault. That we were simply the helpless put-upon victims. But in the end, we are responsible for ourselves. And I guess—I'm not sure—but I want to believe it—that in their own pathetic, *dangerous* way, they just loved us too much.

[*A beat*]

Finis. Applause.

[*DONALD hesitates, walks over to* MICHAEL, *puts his arms around him, and holds him. It is a totally warm and caring gesture*]

There's nothing quite as good as feeling sorry for yourself, is there?

15

DONALD
Nothing.

MICHAEL
[*A la Bette Davis*]
I adore cheap sentiment.
[*Breaks away*]
OK, I'm taking orders for drinks. What'll it be?

DONALD
An extra-dry-Beefeater-martini-on-the-rocks-with-a-twist.

MICHAEL
Coming up.
[*DONALD exits up the stairs into the bath; MICHAEL into the kitchen.
Momentarily, MICHAEL returns, carrying an ice bucket in one hand
and a silver tray of cracked crab in the other, singing "Acapulco" or
"Down Argentine Way" or some other forgotten Grable tune.
The telephone rings*]

MICHAEL
[*Answering it*]
Backstage, *New Moon.*
[*A beat*]
Alan? My God, I don't believe it. How *are* you? *Where* are you? In
town! Great! When'd you get in? Is Fran with you? Oh. What? No.
No, I'm tied up tonight. No, tonight's no good for me.— You mean,
now? Well, Alan, ole boy, it's a friend's birthday and I'm having a
few people.— No, you wouldn't exactly call it a birthday party—
well, yes, actually I guess you would. I mean, what else would you
call it? A *wake*, maybe. I'm sorry I can't ask you to join us—but—
well, kiddo, it just wouldn't work out.— No, it's not place cards or
anything. It's just that—well, I'd hate to just see you for ten minutes and...Alan? Alan? What's the matter?— Are you—are you crying?— Oh, Alan, what's wrong?— Alan, listen, come on over. No,
no, it's perfectly all right. Well, just hurry up. I mean, come on by
and have a drink, OK? Alan...are you all right? OK. Yeah. Same old
address. Yeah. Bye.
[*Slowly hangs up, stares blankly into space. DONALD appears,
bathed and changed. He strikes a pose*]

DONALD
Well. Am I stunning?
[*MICHAEL looks up*]

MICHAEL
    [*Tonelessly*]
You're absolutely stunning.— You *look* like shit, but I'm absolutely
stunned.

DONALD
    [*Crestfallen*]
Your grapes are, how you say, sour.

MICHAEL
Listen, you won't believe what just happened.

DONALD
Where's my drink?

MICHAEL
I didn't make it—I've been on the phone.
    [*DONALD goes to the bar, makes himself a martini*]
My old roommate from Georgetown just called.

DONALD
Alan what's-his-name?

MICHAEL
McCarthy. He's up here from Washington on business or something
and he's on his way over here.

DONALD
Well, I hope he knows the lyrics to "Happy Birthday."

MICHAEL
Listen, asshole, what am I going to do? He's *straight*. And *Square
City!*
    [*"Top Drawer" accent through clenched teeth*]
I mean, he's rally vury proper. Auffully good family.

DONALD
    [*Same accent*]
That's *so* important.

MICHAEL
    [*Regular speech*]
I mean, they look down on people in the *theater*—so whatta you
think he'll feel about this *freak show* I've got booked for dinner?

DONALD
[*Sipping his drink*]
Christ, is that good.

MICHAEL
Want some cracked crab?

DONALD
Not just yet. Why'd you invite him over?

MICHAEL
He invited himself. He said he had to see me tonight. *Immediately.*
He absolutely lost his spring on the phone—started crying.

DONALD
Maybe he's feeling sorry for himself too.

MICHAEL
Great heaves and sobs. Really boo-hoo-hoo-time—and that's not his
style at all. I mean, he's so pulled-together he wouldn't show any
emotion if he were in a plane crash. What am I going to do?

DONALD
What the hell do you care what he thinks?

MICHAEL
Well, I don't really, but…

DONALD
Or are you suddenly ashamed of your friends?

MICHAEL
Donald, *you* are the only person I know of whom I am truly
ashamed. Some people *do* have different standards from yours and
mine, you know. And if we don't acknowledge them, we're just as
narrow-minded and backward as we think they are.

DONALD
You know what you are, Michael? You're a *real* person.

MICHAEL
Thank you and fuck you.
[*MICHAEL crosses to take a piece of crab and nibble on it*]
Want some?

DONALD
No, thanks. How could you ever have been friends with a bore like
that?

MICHAEL
Believe it or not, there was a time in my life when I didn't go
around *announcing* that I was a faggot.

DONALD
That must have been before speech replaced sign language.

MICHAEL
Don't give me any static on that score. I didn't come out until I left
college.

DONALD
It seems to me that the first time we tricked we met in a gay bar on
Third Avenue during your *junior* year.

MICHAEL
Cunt.

DONALD
I thought you'd never say it.

MICHAEL
Sure you don't want any cracked crab?

DONALD
Not yet! If you don't mind!

MICHAEL
Well, it can only be getting colder. What time is it?

DONALD
I don't know. Early.

MICHAEL
Where the hell is Alan?

DONALD
Do you want some more club soda?

MICHAEL
What?

DONALD
There's nothing but club soda in that glass. It's not gin—like mine.
You want some more?

MICHAEL
No.

DONALD
I've been watching you for several Saturdays now. You've actually
stopped drinking, haven't you?

MICHAEL
And smoking too.

DONALD
And smoking too. How long's it been?

MICHAEL
Five weeks.

DONALD
That's amazing.

MICHAEL
I've found God.

DONALD
It *is* amazing—for you.

MICHAEL
Or is God dead?

DONALD
Yes, thank God. And don't get panicky just because I'm paying you
a compliment. I can tell the difference.

MICHAEL
You always said that I held my liquor better than anybody you ever
saw.

DONALD
I could always tell when you were getting high—one way.

MICHAEL
I'd get hostile.

DONALD
You seem happier or something now—and that shows.

MICHAEL
[*Quietly*]
Thanks.

DONALD
What made you stop—the analyst?

MICHAEL
He certainly had a lot to do with it. Mainly, I just didn't think I could survive another hangover, that's all. I don't think I could get through that morning-after ick attack.

DONALD
Morning-after what?

MICHAEL
Icks! Anxiety! Guilt! Unfathomable guilt—either real or imagined—from that split second your eyes pop open and you say, "Oh, my God, what did I do last night!" and ZAP, total recall!

DONALD
Tell me about it!

MICHAEL
Then, the coffee, aspirin, Alka-Seltzer, Darvon, Daprisal, and a quick call to I.A.—Icks Anonymous.

DONALD
"Good morning, I.A."

MICHAEL
"Hi! Was I too bad last night? Did I do anything wrong? I didn't do anything terrible, did I?"

DONALD
[*Laughing*]
How many times! How many times!

MICHAEL *second time he bitches about lifestyle*
And from then on, that struggle to live till lunch, when you have a
double Bloody Mary—that is, if you've *waited* until lunch—and then
you're half pissed again and useless for the rest of the afternoon. And
the only sure cure is to go to bed for about thirty-seven hours, but
who ever does that? Instead, you hang on till cocktail time, and by
then you're ready for what the night holds—which hopefully is
another party, where the whole goddamn cycle starts over!
     [*A beat*]
Well, I've been on that merry-go-round long enough and I either
had to get off or die of centrifugal force.

DONALD
And just how does a clear head stack up with the dull fog of
alcohol?

MICHAEL
Well, all those things you've always heard are true. Nothing can
compare with the experience of one's faculties functioning at their
maximum natural capacity. The only thing is…I'd *kill* for a drink.
     [*The wall-panel buzzer sounds*]

DONALD
Joe College has finally arrived.

MICHAEL
Suddenly, I have such an ick!
     [*Presses the wall-panel button*]
Now listen, Donald…

DONALD
     [*Quick*]
Michael, don't insult me by giving me any lecture on acceptable
social behavior. I promise to sit with my legs spread apart and keep
my voice in a deep register.

MICHAEL
Donald, you are a real *card-carrying cunt*.
     [*The apartment door buzzes several times. MICHAEL goes to it,
     pauses briefly before it, tears it open to reveal EMORY, LARRY, and
     HANK. EMORY is in Bermuda shorts and a sweater. LARRY has on a
     turtleneck and sandals. HANK is in a dark Ivy League suit with a
     vest and has on cordovan shoes. LARRY and HANK carry birthday
     gifts. EMORY carries a large covered dish*]

22

EMORY
[*Bursting in*]
ALL RIGHT THIS IS A RAID! EVERYBODY'S UNDER
ARREST!
[*This entrance is followed by a loud raucous laugh as* EMORY
throws his arms around MICHAEL *and gives him a big kiss on the
cheek.*]
[*Referring to dish*]
Hello, darlin! Connie Casserole. Oh, Mary, don't ask.

MICHAEL
[*Weary already*]
Hello, Emory. Put it in the kitchen.
[EMORY *spots* DONALD]

EMORY
Who is this exotic woman over here?

MICHAEL
Hi, Hank. Larry.
[*They say,"Hi," shake hands, enter.* MICHAEL *looks out in the hall,
comes back into the room, closes the door*]

DONALD
Hi, Emory.

EMORY
My dear, I thought you had perished! Where have you been hiding
your classically chiseled features?

DONALD
[*To* EMORY]
I don't live in the city anymore.

MICHAEL
[*To* LARRY *and* HANK, *referring to the gifts*]
Here, I'll take those. Where's yours, Emory?

EMORY
It's arriving later.
[EMORY *exits to the kitchen.* LARRY *and* DONALD's *eyes have
met.* HANK *has handed* MICHAEL *his gift*—LARRY *is too
preoccupied*]

HANK
Larry!— Larry!

LARRY
What!

HANK
Give Michael the gift!

LARRY
Oh. Here.
     [*To* HANK]
Louder. So my mother in Philadelphia can hear you.

HANK
Well, you were just standing there in a trance.

MICHAEL
     [*To* LARRY *and* HANK *as* EMORY *reenters*]
You both know Donald, don't you?

DONALD
Sure. Nice to see you.
     [*To* HANK]
Hi.

HANK
     [*Shaking hands*]
Nice to meet you.

MICHAEL
Oh, I thought you'd met.

DONALD
Well...

LARRY
We haven't exactly me but we've... Hi.

DONALD
Hi.

HANK
But you've what?

LARRY
...*Seen*...each other before.

MICHAEL
Well, *that* sounds murky.

HANK
You've never met but you've seen each other.

LARRY
What was wrong with the way *I* said it?

HANK
Where?

EMORY
[*Loud aside to* MICHAEL]
I think they're going to have their first fight.

LARRY
The first one since we got out of the taxi.

MICHAEL
[*Referring to* EMORY]
Where'd you find this trash?

LARRY
Downstairs leaning against a lamppost.

EMORY
With an orchid behind my ear and big wet lips painted over the lipline.

MICHAEL
Just like Maria Montez.

DONALD
Oh, *please!*

EMORY
[*To* DONALD]
What have you got against Maria—she was a good woman.

MICHAEL
Listen, everybody, this old college friend of mine is in town and he's stopping by for a fast drink on his way to dinner somewhere. But, listen, he's *straight,* so…

LARRY
Straight! If it's the one I met, he's about as straight as the Yellow Brick Road.

MICHAEL
No, you met Justin Stuart.

HANK
I don't remember anybody named Justin Stuart.

LARRY
Of course you don't, dope. *I* met him.

MICHAEL
Well, this is someone else.

DONALD
Alan McCarthy. A very close total stranger.

MICHAEL
It's not that I care what he would think of me, really—it's just that
he's not ready for it. And he never will be. You understand that,
don't you, Hank?

HANK
Oh, sure.

LARRY
You honestly think he doesn't know about you?

MICHAEL
If there's the slightest suspicion, he's never let on one bit.

EMORY
What's he had, a lobotomy?
    [*He exits up the stairs into the bath*]

MICHAEL
I was super-careful when I was in college and I still am whenever I
see him. I don't know why, but I am.

DONALD
Tilt.

MICHAEL
You may think it was a crock of shit, Donald, but to him I'm sure
we were close friends. The closest. To pop that balloon now just
wouldn't be fair to him. Isn't that right?

26

LARRY
Whatever's fair.

MICHAEL
Well, of course. And if that's phony of me, Donald, then that's
phony of me and make something of it.

DONALD
I pass.

MICHAEL
Well, even you have to admit it's much simpler to deal with
the world according to its rules and then go right ahead and
do what you damn well please. You do understand *that*, don't
you?

DONALD
Now that you've put it in layman's terms.

MICHAEL
I was just like Alan when I was in college. Very large in the dating
department. Wore nothing but those constipated Ivy League
clothes and those ten-pound cordovan shoes.
        [*To* HANK]
No offense.

HANK
Quite all right.

MICHAEL
I butched it up quite a bit. And I didn't think I was lying to myself.
I really thought I was straight.

EMORY
        [*Coming downstairs tucking a Kleenex into his sleeve*]
Who do you have to fuck to get a drink around here?

MICHAEL
Will you *light* somewhere?
        [*EMORY sits on steps*]
Or I thought I thought I was straight. I know I didn't come out till
after I'd graduated.

DONALD
What about all those weekends up from school?

MICHAEL
I still wasn't out. I was still in the "Christ-was-I-drunk-last-night syndrome."

LARRY
The *what?*

MICHAEL
The Christ-was-I-drunk-last-night syndrome. You know, when you made it with some guy in school, and the next day when you had to face each other there was always a lot of shit-kicking crap about, "Man, was I drunk last night! Christ, I don't remember a thing!"
[*Everyone laughs*]

DONALD
You were just guilty because you were Catholic, that's all.

MICHAEL
That's not true. The Christ-was-I-drunk-last-night syndrome knows no religion. It has to do with immaturity. Although I will admit there's a high percentage of it among Mormons.

EMORY
Trollop.

MICHAEL
We all somehow managed to justify our actions in those days. I later found out that even Justin Stuart, my closest friend…

DONALD
Other than Alan McCarthy.

MICHAEL
[*A look to DONALD*]
…was doing the same thing. Only Justin was going to Boston on weekends.
[*EMORY and LARRY laugh*]

LARRY
[*To HANK*]
Sound familiar?

MICHAEL
Yes, long before Justin and I or God only knows how many others *came out*, we used to get drunk and "horse around" a bit. You see, in the Christ-was-I-drunk-last-night syndrome, you really *are* drunk. That part of it is true. It's just that you also *do remember everything*.
  [*General laughter*]
Oh, God, I used to have to get loaded to go in a gay bar!

DONALD
Well, times certainly have changed.

MICHAEL
They *have*. Lately I've gotten to despise the bars. Everybody just standing around and standing around—it's like one eternal intermission.

HANK
  [*To LARRY*]
Sound familiar?

EMORY
I can't stand the bars either. All that cat-and-mouse business—you hang around *staring* at each other all night and wind up going home alone.

MICHAEL
And pissed.

LARRY
A lot of guys have to get loaded to have sex.
  [*Quick look to HANK, who is unamused*]
So I've been told.

MICHAEL
If you remember, Donald, the first time we made it I was so drunk I could hardly stand up.

DONALD
You were so drunk you could hardly *get* it up.

MICHAEL
  [*Mock innocence*]
Christ, I was so drunk I don't remember.

DONALD
Bullshit, you remember.

MICHAEL
[*Sings to* DONALD]
"Just friends, lovers no more…"

EMORY
You may as well be. Everybody thinks you are anyway.

DONALD
We never *were—really.*

MICHAEL
We didn't have time to be—we got to know each other too fast.
[*Door buzzer sounds*]
Oh, Jesus, it's Alan! Now, please, everybody, do me a favor and cool
it for the few minutes he's here.

EMORY
Anything for a sis, Mary.

MICHAEL
That's *exactly* what I'm talking about, Emory. *No camping!*

EMORY
Sorry.
[*Deep, deep voice to* DONALD]
Think the Giants are gonna win the pennant this year?

DONALD
[*Deep, deep voice*]
Fuckin' A, Mac.
[MICHAEL *goes to the door, opens it to reveal* BERNARD, *dressed in a
shirt and tie and sport jacket. He carries a birthday gift and two
bottles of red wine*]

EMORY
[*Big scream*]
Oh, it's only another queen!

BERNARD
And it ain't the red one, either.

EMORY
It's the queen of spades!
[BERNARD *enters.* MICHAEL *looks out in the hall*]

30

MICHAEL
Bernard, is the downstairs door open?

BERNARD
It was, but I closed it.

MICHAEL
Good.
[*BERNARD starts to put wine on bar*]

MICHAEL
[*Referring to the two bottles of red wine*]
I'll take those. You can put your present with the others.
[*MICHAEL closes the door. BERNARD hands him the gift. The phone rings*]

BERNARD
Hi, Larry. Hi, Hank.

MICHAEL
Christ of the Andes! Donald, will you bartend, please?
[*MICHAEL gives DONALD the wine bottles, goes to the phone*]

BERNARD
[*Extending his hand to DONALD*]
Hello, Donald. Good to see you.

DONALD
Bernard.

MICHAEL
[*Answers phone*]
Hello? Alan?

EMORY
Hi, Bernardette. Anybody ever tell you you'd look divine in a hammock, surrounded by louvres and ceiling fans and lots and lots of lush tropical ferns?

BERNARD
[*To EMORY*]
You're *such* a fag. You take the cake.

EMORY
Oh, what *about* the cake—whose job was that?

LARRY
Mine. I ordered one to be delivered.

EMORY
How many candles did you say put on it—eighty?

MICHAEL
…What? Wait a minute. There's too much noise. Let me go to another
phone.
[*Presses the hold button, hangs up, dashes toward stairs*]

LARRY
Michael, did the cake come?

MICHAEL
No.

DONALD
[*To MICHAEL as he passes*]
What's up?

MICHAEL
Do *I* know?

LARRY
Jesus, I'd better call. OK if I use the private line?

MICHAEL
[*Going upstairs*]
Sure.
[*Stops dead on stairs, turns*]
Listen, everybody, there's some cracked crab there. Help yourselves.
[*DONALD shakes his head. MICHAEL continues up the stairs to the
bedroom. LARRY crosses to the phone, presses the free-line button,
picks up receiver, dials information*]

DONALD
Is everybody ready for a drink?
[*HANK and BERNARD say, "Yeah"*]

EMORY
[*Flipping up his sweater*]
Ready! I'll be your topless cocktail waitress.

BERNARD
Please spare us the sight of your sagging tits.

EMORY
[*To* HANK, LARRY]
What're you having, kids?

MICHAEL
[*Having picked up the bedside phone*]
...Yes, Alan...

LARRY
Vodka and tonic.
[*Into phone*]
Could I have the number for the Marseilles Bakery in Manhattan?

EMORY
A vod and ton and a...

HANK
Is there any beer?

EMORY
Beer! Who drinks beer before dinner?

BERNARD
Beer drinkers.

DONALD
That's telling him.

MICHAEL
...No, Alan, don't be silly. What's there to apologize for?

EMORY
Truck drivers do. Or...or wallpaperers. Not schoolteachers. They have sherry.

HANK
This one has beer.

EMORY
Well, maybe schoolteachers in *public* schools.
[*To* LARRY]
How can a sensitive artist like you live with an insensitive bull like that?

LARRY
[*Hanging up the phone and redialing*]
I can't.

BERNARD
Emory, you'd live with Hank in a minute, if he'd ask you. In fifty-eight seconds. Lord knows, you're *sss*ensitive.

EMORY
Why don't you have a piece of watermelon and hush up!

MICHAEL
...Alan, don't be ridiculous.

DONALD
Here you go, Hank.

HANK
Thanks.

LARRY
Shit. They don't answer.

DONALD
What're you having, Emory?

BERNARD
A Pink Lady.

EMORY
A vodka martini on the rocks, please.

LARRY
        [*Hangs up*]
Well, let's just hope.
        [*DONALD hands LARRY his drink—their eyes meet again. A faint smile crosses LARRY's lips. DONALD returns to the bar to make EMORY's drink*]

MICHAEL
Lunch tomorrow will be great. One o'clock—the Oak Room at the Plaza OK? Fine.

BERNARD
        [*To DONALD*]
Donald, read any new libraries lately?

DONALD
One or three. I did the complete works of Doris Lessing this week. I've been depressed.

MICHAEL
Alan, forget it, will you? Right. Bye.
  [*Hangs up, starts to leave the room—stops. Quickly pulls off the
  sweater he is wearing, takes out another, crosses to the stairs*]

DONALD
You must not work in Circulation anymore.

BERNARD
Oh, I'm still there—every day.

DONALD
Well, since I moved, I only come in on Saturday evenings.
  [*Moves his stack of books off the bar*]

HANK
Looks like you stock up for the week.
  [MICHAEL *rises and crosses to steps landing*]

BERNARD
Are you kidding?—that'll last him two days.

EMORY
It would last *me* two years. I still haven't finished *Atlas Shrugged*,
which I started in 1912.

MICHAEL
  [*To* DONALD]
Well, he's not coming.

DONALD
It's just as well now.

BERNARD
Some people eat, some people drink, some take dope…

DONALD
I read.

MICHAEL
And read and read and read. It's a wonder your eyes don't turn back
in your head at the sight of a dust jacket.

HANK
Well, at least he's a constructive escapist.

MICHAEL
Yeah, what do I do?—take planes. No, I don't do that anymore.
Because I don't have the *money* to do that anymore. I go to the
baths. That's about it.

EMORY
I'm about to do both. I'm flying to the West Coast—

BERNARD
You still have that act with a donkey in Tijuana?

EMORY
I'm going to *San Francisco* on a well-earned vacation.

LARRY
No shopping?

EMORY
Oh, I'll look for a few things for a couple of clients, but I've been so
busy lately I really couldn't care less if I never saw another piece of
fabric or another stick of furniture as long as I live. I'm going to the
Club Baths and I'm not out till they announce the departure of
TWA one week later.

BERNARD
[*To* EMORY]
You'll never learn to stay out of the baths, will you? The last time
Emily was taking the vapors, this big hairy number strolled in. Emory
said, "I'm just resting," and the big hairy number said, "I'm just
*ar*resting!" It was the vice!
[*Everybody laughs*]

EMORY
You have to tell everything, don't you!
[*DONALD crosses to give* EMORY *his drink*]
Thanks, sonny. You live with your parents?

DONALD
Yeah. But it's all right—they're gay.
[*EMORY roars, slaps* HANK *on the knee.* HANK *gets up, moves away.*
DONALD *turns to* MICHAEL]
What happened to Alan?

36

MICHAEL
He suddenly got terrible icks about having broken down on the phone. Kept apologizing over and over. Did a big about-face and reverted to the old Alan right before my very eyes.

DONALD
Ears.

MICHAEL
Ears. Well, the cracked crab obviously did not work out.
     [*Starts to take away the tray*]

EMORY
Just put that down if you don't want your hand slapped. I'm about to have some.

MICHAEL
It's really very good.
     [*Gives* DONALD *a look*]
I don't know why everyone has such an aversion to it.

DONALD
Sometimes you remind me of the Chinese water torture. I take that back. Sometimes you remind me of the *relentless* Chinese water torture.

MICHAEL
Bitch.
     [HANK *has put on some music*]

BERNARD
Yeah, baby, let's hear that sound.

EMORY
A drumbeat and their eyes sparkle like Cartier's.
     [BERNARD *starts to snap his fingers and move in time with the music.* MICHAEL *joins in*]

HANK
I wonder where Harold is.

EMORY
Yeah, where *is* the frozen fruit?

MICHAEL
     [*To* DONALD]
Emory refers to Harold as the frozen fruit because of his former profession as an ice skater.

EMORY
She used to be the Vera Hruba Ralston of the Borscht Circuit.
[*MICHAEL and BERNARD are now dancing freely*]

BERNARD
[*To MICHAEL*]
If your mother could see you now, she'd have a stroke.

MICHAEL
Got a camera on you?
[*The door panel buzzes. EMORY lets out a yelp*]

EMORY
Oh, my God, it's Lily Law! Everybody three feet apart!
[*MICHAEL goes to the panel, presses the button. HANK turns down
the music. MICHAEL opens the door a short way, pokes his head
out*]

BERNARD
It's probably Harold now.
[*MICHAEL leans back in the room*]

MICHAEL
No, it's the delivery boy from the bakery.

LARRY
Thank God.
[*MICHAEL goes out into the hall, pulling the door almost closed
behind him*]

EMORY
[*Loudly*]
Ask him if he's got any hot cross buns!

HANK
Come on, Emory, knock it off.

BERNARD
You can take her anywhere but out.

EMORY
[*To HANK*]
You remind me of an old-maid schoolteacher.

HANK
You remind me of a chicken wing.

38

EMORY
I'm sure you meant that as a compliment.
    [HANK *turns the music back up*]

MICHAEL
    [*In hall*]
Thank you. Good night.
    [MICHAEL *returns with a cake box, closes the door, and takes it into the kitchen*]

LARRY
Hey, Bernard, you remember that thing we used to do on Fire Island?
    [LARRY *starts to do a kind of Madison*]

BERNARD
That was "in" so far back I think I've forgotten.

EMORY
I remember.
    [*Pops up—starts doing the steps.* LARRY *and* BERNARD *start to follow*]

LARRY
Yeah. That's it.
    [MICHAEL *enters from the kitchen, falls in line with them*]

MICHAEL
Well, if it isn't the Geriatrics Rockettes.
    [*Now they all are doing practically a precision routine.* DONALD *comes to sit on the arm of a chair, sip his drink, and watch in fascination.* HANK *goes to the bar to get another beer. The door buzzer sounds. No one seems to hear it. It buzzes again.* HANK *turns toward the door, hesitates. Looks toward* MICHAEL, *who is now deeply involved in the intricacies of the dance. No one, it seems, has heard the buzzer but* HANK, *who goes to the door, opens it wide to reveal* ALAN. *He is dressed in black tie. The dancers continue, turning and slapping their knees and heels and laughing with abandon. Suddenly* MICHAEL *looks up, stops dead.* DONALD *sees this and turns to see what* MICHAEL *has seen. Slowly he stands up.* MICHAEL *goes to the record player, turns it off abruptly.* EMORY, LARRY, *and* BERNARD *come to out-of-step halts, look to see what's happened*]

MICHAEL
I thought you said you weren't coming.

ALAN
I...well, I'm sorry...

MICHAEL
[*Forced lightly*]
We were just—acting silly...

ALAN
Actually, when I called I was in a phone booth around the corner.
My dinner party is not far from here. And...

MICHAEL
Emory was just showing us this...silly dance.

ALAN
Well, then I walked past and your downstairs door was open and...

MICHAEL
This is Emory.
    [*EMORY curtsies. MICHAEL glares at him*]
Everybody, this is Alan McCarthy. Counterclockwise, Alan: Larry,
Emory, Bernard, Donald, and Hank.
    [*They all mumble "Hello," "Hi"*]
Would you like a drink?

ALAN
Thanks, no. I...I can't stay...long...really.

MICHAEL
Well, you're here now, so stay. What would you like?

ALAN
Do you have any rye?   *No gay man has ever drunk rye*

MICHAEL
I'm afraid I don't drink it anymore. You'll have to settle for gin or Scotch
or vodka.

DONALD
Or beer.

40

ALAN
Scotch, please.
        [MICHAEL starts for bar]

DONALD
I'll get it.
        [Goes to bar]

HANK
        [Forced laugh]
Guess I'm the only beer drinker.

ALAN
        [Looking around group]
Whose...birthday...is it?

LARRY
Harold's.

ALAN
        [Looking from face to face]
Harold?

BERNARD
He's not here yet.

EMORY
She's never been on time...
        [MICHAEL shoots EMORY a withering glance]
He's never been on time in his...

MICHAEL
Alan's from Washington. We went to college together. Georgetown.
        [A beat. Silence]

EMORY
Well, isn't that fascinating.
        [DONALD hands ALAN his drink]

DONALD
If that's too strong, I'll put some water in it.

ALAN
        [Takes a quick gulp]
It's fine. Thanks. Fine.

HANK
Are you in the government?

ALAN
No. I'm a lawyer. What...what do you do?

HANK
I teach school.

ALAN
Oh. I would have taken you for an athlete of some sort. You look
like you might play sports...of some sort.

HANK
Well, I'm no professional but I was on the basketball team in college and I play quite a bit of tennis.

ALAN
I play tennis too.

HANK
Great game.

ALAN
Yes. Great.
        [*A beat. Silence*]
What...do you teach?

HANK
Math.

ALAN
Math?

HANK
Yes.

ALAN
Math. Well.

EMORY
Kinda makes you want to rush out and buy a slide rule, doesn't it?

MICHAEL
Emory. I'm going to need some help with dinner and you're elected.
Come on!

42

EMORY
I'm *always* elected.

BERNARD
You're a natural-born domestic.

EMORY
Said the African queen! You come on too—you can fan me while I
make the salad dressing.

MICHAEL
[*Glaring. Phony smile*]
RIGHT THIS WAY, EMORY!
[*MICHAEL pushes the swinging door aside for EMORY and BERNARD
to enter. They do and he follows. The door swings closed, and the
muffled sound of MICHAEL's voice can be heard.
Offstage*]
You son of a bitch!

EMORY
[*Offstage*]
What the hell do you want from me?

HANK
Why don't we all sit down?

ALAN
...Sure.
[*HANK and ALAN sit on the couch. LARRY crosses to the bar, refills his
drink. DONALD comes over to refill his*]

LARRY
Hi.

DONALD
...Hi.

ALAN
I really feel terrible—barging in on you fellows this way.

LARRY
[*To DONALD*]
How've you been?

DONALD
Fine, thanks.

HANK
  [*To ALAN*]
…Oh, that's OK.

DONALD
  [*To LARRY*]
…And you?

LARRY
Oh…just fine.

ALAN
  [*To HANK*]
You're married?
  [*LARRY hears this, turns to look in the direction of the couch.
  MICHAEL enters from the kitchen*]

HANK
  [*Watching LARRY and DONALD*]
What?

ALAN
I see you're married.
  [*Points to HANK's wedding band*]

HANK
Oh.

MICHAEL
  [*Glaring at DONALD*]
Yes. Hank's married.

ALAN
You have any kids?

HANK
Yes. Two. A boy, nine, and a girl, seven. You should see my boy play
tennis—really puts his dad to shame.

DONALD
  [*Avoiding MICHAEL's eyes*]
I better get some ice.
  [*Exits to the kitchen*]

ALAN
[*To* HANK]
I have two kids too. Both girls.

HANK
Great.

MICHAEL
How are the girls, Alan?

ALAN
Oh, just sensational.
[*Shakes his head*]
They're something, those kids. God, I'm nuts about them.

HANK
How long have you been married?

ALAN
Nine years. Can you believe it, Mickey?

MICHAEL
No.

ALAN
Mickey used to go with my wife when we were all in school.

MICHAEL
Can you believe that?

ALAN
[*To* HANK]
You live in the city?

LARRY
Yes, we do.
[*LARRY comes over to couch next to* HANK]

ALAN
Oh.

HANK
I'm in the process of getting a divorce. Larry and I are—roommates.

MICHAEL
Yes.

ALAN
Oh. I'm sorry. Oh, I mean...

HANK
I understand.

ALAN
[*Gets up*]
I...I...I think I'd like another drink...if I may.

MICHAEL
Of course. What was it?

ALAN
I'll do it...if I may.
        [*Gets up, starts for the bar. Suddenly there is a loud crash offstage.*
        ALAN *jumps, looks toward swinging door*]
What was that?
        [DONALD *enters with the ice bucket*]

MICHAEL
Excuse me. Testy temperament out in the kitch!
        [MICHAEL *exits through the swinging door.* ALAN *continues to the
        bar—starts nervously picking up and putting down bottles, searching
        for the Scotch*]

HANK
[*To* LARRY]
Larry, where do you know that guy from?

LARRY
What guy?

HANK
That guy.

LARRY
I don't know. Around. The bars.

DONALD
Can I help you, Alan?

ALAN
I...I can't seem to find the Scotch.

DONALD
You've got it in your hand.

ALAN
Oh. Of course. How...stupid of me.
    [*DONALD watches* ALAN *fumble with the Scotch bottle and glass*]

DONALD
Why don't you let me do that?

ALAN
    [*Gratefully hands him both*]
Thanks.

DONALD
Was it water or soda?

ALAN
Just make it straight—over ice.
    [MICHAEL *enters*]

MICHAEL
You see, Alan, I told you it wasn't a good time to talk. But we...

ALAN
It doesn't matter. I'll just finish this and go...
    [*Takes a long swallow*]

LARRY
Where can Harold be?

MICHAEL
Oh, he's always late. You know how neurotic he is about going out
in public. It takes him hours to get ready.

LARRY
Why *is* that?
    [EMORY *breezes in with an apron tied around his waist, carrying a
    stack of plates, which he places on a drop-leaf table.* MICHAEL *does
    an eye roll*]

EMORY
Why is what?

LARRY
Why does Harold spend hours getting ready before he can go out?

EMORY
Because she's a sick lady, that's why.
          [*Exits to the kitchen.* ALAN *finishes his drink*]

MICHAEL
Alan, as I was about to say, we can go in the bedroom and talk.

ALAN
It really doesn't matter.

MICHAEL
Come on. Bring your drink.

ALAN
I...I've finished it.

MICHAEL
Well, make another and bring it upstairs.
          [DONALD *picks up the Scotch bottle and pours into the glass* ALAN
          has in his hand. MICHAEL *has started for the stairs*]

ALAN
          [*To* DONALD]
Thanks.

DONALD
Don't mention it.

ALAN
          [*To* HANK]
Excuse me. We'll be down in a minute.

LARRY
He'll still be here.
          [*A beat*]

MICHAEL
          [*On the stairs*]
Go ahead, Alan. I'll be right there.

          [ALAN *turns awkwardly, exits to the bedroom.* MICHAEL *goes into the
          kitchen. A beat*]

HANK
          [*To* LARRY]
What was *that* supposed to mean?

LARRY
What was what supposed to mean?

HANK
You know.

LARRY
You want another beer?

HANK
No. You're jealous, aren't you?
        [HANK starts to laugh. LARRY doesn't like it]

LARRY
I'm Larry. *You're* jealous.
        [*Crosses to* DONALD]
Hey, Donald, where've you been hanging out these days? I haven't
seen you in a long time...
        [MICHAEL *enters to witness this disapprovingly. He turns, goes up the*
        stairs. In the bedroom ALAN *is sitting on the edge of the bed.* MICHAEL
        enters, pauses at the mirror to adjust his hair. Downstairs, HANK *gets*
        up, exits into the kitchen. DONALD *and* LARRY *move to a corner of the*
        room, sit facing upstage, and talk quietly]

ALAN
        [*To* MICHAEL]
This is a marvelous apartment.

MICHAEL
It's too expensive. I work to pay rent.

ALAN
What are you doing these days?

MICHAEL
Nothing.

ALAN
Aren't you writing anymore?

MICHAEL
I haven't looked at a typewriter since I sold the very, very
wonderful, very, very marvelous *screenplay*, which never got
produced.

ALAN
That's right. The last time I saw you, you were on your way to
California. Or was it Europe?

MICHAEL
Hollywood. Which is not in Europe, nor does it have anything
whatsoever to do with California.

ALAN
I've never been there, but I would imagine it's awful. Everyone
must be terribly cheap.

MICHAEL
No, not everyone.
   [*ALAN laughs. A beat. MICHAEL sits on the bed*]
Alan, I want to try to explain this evening…

ALAN
What's there to explain? Sometimes you just can't invite everybody
to every party and some people take it personally. But I'm not one
of them. I should apologize for inviting myself.

MICHAEL
That's not exactly what I meant.

ALAN
Your friends all seem like very nice guys. That Hank is really a very
attractive fellow.

MICHAEL
…Yes. He is.

ALAN
We have a lot in common. What's his roommate's name?

MICHAEL
Larry.

ALAN
What does *he* do?

MICHAEL
He's a commercial artist.

ALAN

I liked Donald too. The only one I didn't care too much for was—
what's his name—Emory?

MICHAEL

Yes. Emory.

ALAN

I just can't stand that kind of talk. It just grates on me.

MICHAEL

What kind of talk, Alan?

ALAN

Oh, you know. His brand of humor, I guess.

MICHAEL

He can be really quite funny sometimes.

ALAN

I suppose so. If you find that sort of thing amusing. He just seems
like such a goddamn little pansy.
[Silence. A pause]
I'm sorry I said that. I didn't mean to say that. That's such an awful
thing to say about *anyone*. But you know what I mean, Michael—
you have to admit he *is* effeminate.

MICHAEL

He is a bit.

ALAN

A bit! He's like a…a butterfly in heat! I mean, there's no wonder he
was trying to teach you all a dance. He *probably* wanted to dance
with you!
[Pause]
Oh, come on, man, you know me—you know how I feel—your private life is your own affair.

MICHAEL

[Icy]
No. I *don't* know that about you.

ALAN

I couldn't care less what people do—as long as they don't do it in
public—or—or try to force their ways on the whole damned world.

MICHAEL
Alan, what was it you were crying about on the telephone?

ALAN
Oh, I feel like such a fool about that. I could shoot myself for letting myself act that way. I'm so embarrassed I could die.

MICHAEL
But, Alan, if you were genuinely upset—that's nothing to be embarrassed about.

ALAN
All I can say is—please accept my apology for making such an ass of myself.

MICHAEL
You must have been upset, or you wouldn't have said you were and that you wanted to see me—*had* to see me and had to talk to me.

ALAN
Can you forget it? Just pretend it never happened. I know *I* have. OK?

MICHAEL
Is something wrong between you and Fran?

ALAN
Listen, I've really got to go.

MICHAEL
Why are you in New York?

ALAN
I'm dreadfully late for dinner.

MICHAEL
Whose dinner? Where are you going?

ALAN
Is this the loo?

MICHAEL
Yes.

ALAN
Excuse me.
> [*Quickly goes into the bathroom, closes the door. MICHAEL remains silent—sits on the bed, stares into space. Downstairs, EMORY pops in from the kitchen to discover DONALD and LARRY in quiet, intimate conversation*]

EMORY
What's-going-on-in-here-oh-Mary-don't-ask!
> [*Puts a salt cellar and pepper mill on the table. HANK enters, carrying a bottle of red wine and a corkscrew. Looks toward LARRY and DONALD. DONALD sees him, stands up*]

DONALD
Hank, why don't you come and join us?

HANK
That's an interesting suggestion. Whose idea is that?

DONALD
Mine.

LARRY
> [*To HANK*]
He means in a conversation.
> [*BERNARD enters from the kitchen, carrying four wineglasses*]

EMORY
> [*To BERNARD*]
Where're the rest of the wineglasses?

BERNARD
Ahz workin' as fas' as ah can!

EMORY
They have to be told everything. Can't let 'em out of your sight.
> [*Breezes out to the kitchen. DONALD leaves LARRY's side and goes to the coffee table, helps himself to the cracked crab. HANK opens the wine, puts it on the table. MICHAEL gets up from the bed and goes down the stairs. Downstairs, HANK crosses to LARRY*]

HANK
I thought maybe you were abiding by the agreement.

LARRY
We have no agreement.

HANK
We *did*.

LARRY
You did. I never agreed to anything!
[*DONALD looks up to see MICHAEL, raises a crab claw toward him*]

DONALD
To your health.

MICHAEL
Up yours.

DONALD
Up my health?

BERNARD
Where's the gent?

MICHAEL
In the gent's room. If you can all hang on five more minutes, he's about to leave.
[*The door buzzes. MICHAEL crosses to it*]

LARRY
Well, at last!
[*MICHAEL opens the door to reveal a muscle-bound young man wearing boots, tight Levi's, a calico neckerchief, and a cowboy hat. Around his wrist there is a large card tied with a ribbon*]

COWBOY
[*Singing fast*]
"Happy birthday to you,
Happy birthday to you,
Happy birthday, dear Harold.
Happy birthday to you."
[*And with that, he throws his arms around MICHAEL and gives him a big kiss on the lips. Everyone stands in stunned silence*]

MICHAEL
Who the hell are you?
[*EMORY swings in from the kitchen*]

EMORY
She's Harold's present from me and she's *early!*
[*Quick, to* COWBOY]
And that's not even Harold, you *idiot!*

COWBOY
You said whoever answered the door.

EMORY
But *not until midnight!*
[*Quickly, to group*]
He's supposed to be a *midnight cowboy!*

DONALD
He *is* a midnight cowboy.

MICHAEL
He looks right out of a William Inge play to me.

EMORY
[*To* COWBOY]
…Not until midnight and you're supposed to sing to the right person, for Chrissake! I *told* you Harold has very, very tight, tight, black curly hair.
[*Referring to* MICHAEL]
This number's practically bald!

MICHAEL
Thank you and fuck you.

BERNARD
It's a good thing *I* didn't open the door.

EMORY
Not that tight and not that black.

COWBOY
I forgot. Besides, I wanted to get to the bars by midnight.

MICHAEL
He's a class act all the way around.

EMORY
What do you mean—get to the bars! Sweetie, I paid you for the whole night, remember?

COWBOY
I hurt my back doing my exercises and I wanted to get to bed early
tonight.

BERNARD
Are you ready for this one?

LARRY
        [*To* COWBOY]
That's too bad, what happened?

COWBOY
I lost my grip doing my chin-ups and I fell on my heels and twisted
my back.

EMORY
You shouldn't *wear* heels when you do chin-ups.

COWBOY
        [*Oblivious*]
I shouldn't do chin-ups—I got a weak grip to begin with.

EMORY
A weak grip. In my day it used to be called a limp wrist.

BERNARD
Who can remember that far back?

MICHAEL
Who was it that always used to say, "You show me Oscar Wilde in a
cowboy suit, and I'll show you a gay caballero."

DONALD
I don't know. Who *was* it who always used to say that?

MICHAEL
        [*Katharine Hepburn voice*]
I don't know. Somebody.

LARRY
        [*To* COWBOY]
What does your card say?

COWBOY
        [*Holds up his wrist*]
Here. Read it.

LARRY
[*Reading card*]
"Dear Harold, bang, bang, you're alive. But roll over and play dead.
Happy birthday, Emory."

BERNARD
Ah, sheer poetry, Emmy.

LARRY
And in your usual good taste.

MICHAEL
Yes, so conservative of you to resist a sign in Times Square.

EMORY
[*Glancing toward stairs*]
Cheese it! Here comes the socialite nun.

MICHAEL
Goddamn it, Emory!
[ALAN *comes down the stairs into the room. Everybody quiets*]

ALAN
Well, I'm off... Thanks, Michael, for the drink.

MICHAEL
You're entirely welcome, Alan. See you tomorrow?

ALAN
...No. No, I think I'm going to be awfully busy. I may even go back
to Washington.

EMORY
Got a heavy date in Lafayette Square?

ALAN
What?

HANK
Emory.

EMORY
Forget it.

ALAN
[*Sees* COWBOY]
Are you...Harold?

EMORY
No, he's not Harold. He's *for* Harold.
    [*Silence.* ALAN *lets it pass. Turns to* HANK]

ALAN
Goodbye, Hank. It was nice to meet you.

HANK
Same here.
    [*They shake hands*]

ALAN
If…if you're ever in Washington—I'd like for you to meet my wife.

LARRY
That'd be fun, wouldn't it, Hank?

EMORY
Yeah, they'd love to meet him—*her.* I have such a problem with pro-nouns.

ALAN
    [*Quick, to* EMORY]
How many esses are there in the word pronoun?

EMORY
How'd you like to kiss my ass—that's got two or more *essessss* in it!

ALAN
How'd you like to blow me!

EMORY
What's the matter with your *wife*, she got lockjaw?

ALAN
    [*Lashes out*]
Faggot, fairy, pansy…
    [*Lunges at* EMORY]
…queer, cocksucker! I'll kill you, you goddamn little mincing swish! You goddamn freak! FREAK! FREAK!
    [*Pandemonium.* ALAN *beats* EMORY *to the floor before anyone recovers from surprise and reacts*]

EMORY
Oh, my God, somebody help me! Bernard! He's killing me!

[*BERNARD and HANK rush forward. EMORY is screaming. Blood gushes from his nose*]

HANK
Alan! ALAN! ALAN!

EMORY
Get him off me! Get him off me! Oh, my God, he's broken my nose! I'm BLEEDING TO DEATH!
[*Larry has gone to shut the door. With one great, athletic move, HANK forcefully tears ALAN off EMORY and drags him backward across the room. BERNARD bends over EMORY, puts his arm around him, and lifts him*]

BERNARD
Somebody get some ice! And a cloth!
[*LARRY runs to the bar, grabs the bar towel and the ice bucket, rushes to put it on the floor beside BERNARD and EMORY. BERNARD quickly wraps some ice in the towel, holds it to EMORY's mouth*]

EMORY
Oh, my face!

BERNARD
He busted your lip, that's all. It'll be all right.
[*HANK has gotten ALAN down on the floor on the opposite side of the room. ALAN relinquishes the struggle, collapses against HANK, moaning and beating his fists rhythmically against HANK's chest. MICHAEL is still standing in the same spot in the center of the room, immobile. DONALD crosses past the COWBOY*]

DONALD
[*To COWBOY*]
Would you mind waiting over there with the gifts?
[*COWBOY moves over to where the gift-wrapped packages have been put. DONALD continues past to observe the mayhem, turns up his glass, takes a long swallow. The door buzzes, DONALD turns toward MICHAEL, waits. MICHAEL doesn't move. DONALD goes to the door, opens it to reveal HAROLD*]
Well, Harold! Happy birthday. You're just in time for the floor show, which, as you see, is on the floor.
[*To COWBOY*]
Hey, you, *this* is Harold!
[*HAROLD looks blankly toward MICHAEL. MICHAEL looks back blankly*]

COWBOY
    [*Crossing to* HAROLD]
"Happy birthday to you,
Happy birthday to you,
Happy birthday, dear Harold.
Happy birthday to you."
    [*Throws his arms around* HAROLD *and gives him a big kiss.* DON-
ALD *looks toward* MICHAEL, *who observes this stoically.* HAROLD
breaks away from COWBOY, *reads the card, begins to laugh.*
MICHAEL *turns to survey the room.* DONALD *watches him. Slowly*
MICHAEL *begins to move. Walks over to the bar, pours a glass of
gin, raises it to his lips, downs it all.* DONALD *watches silently as*
HAROLD *laughs and laughs and laughs*]

CURTAIN

END OF ACT 1

Act 2

A moment later. HAROLD *is still laughing.* MICHAEL, *still at the bar, lowers his glass, turns to* HAROLD.

MICHAEL
What's so fucking funny?

HAROLD
    [*Unintimidated. Quick hand to hip*]
Life. Life is a goddamn laff-riot. You remember life.

MICHAEL
You're stoned. It shows in your arm.

LARRY
Happy birthday, Harold.

MICHAEL
    [*To* HAROLD]
You're stoned and you're late! You were supposed to arrive at this location at approximately eight-thirty dash nine o'clock!

HAROLD
What I *am*, Michael, is a thirty-two-year-old, ugly, pockmarked Jew fairy—and if it takes me a while to pull myself together and if I smoke a little grass before I can get up the nerve to show this face to the world, it's nobody's goddamn business but my own.
    [*Instant switch to chatty tone*]
And how are *you* this evening?
    [HANK *lifts* ALAN *to the couch.* MICHAEL *turns away from* HAROLD, *pours himself another drink.* DONALD *watches.* HAROLD *sweeps past* MICHAEL *over to where* BERNARD *is helping* EMORY *up off the floor.* LARRY *returns the bucket to the bar.* MICHAEL *puts some ice in his drink*]

EMORY
Happy birthday, Hallie.

HAROLD
What happened to *you?*

EMORY
    [*Groans*]
Don't ask!

HAROLD
Your lips are turning blue; you look like you been rimming a snow-man.

EMORY
That piss-elegant kooze hit me!
[*Indicates* ALAN. HAROLD *looks toward the couch.* ALAN *has slumped his head forward into his own lap*]

MICHAEL
Careful, Emory, that kind of talk just makes him s'nervous.
[ALAN *covers his ears with his hands*]

HAROLD
Who is she? Who was she? Who does she hope to be?

EMORY
Who knows, who cares!

HANK
His name is Alan McCarthy.

MICHAEL
Do forgive me for not formally introducing you.

HAROLD
[*Sarcastically, to* MICHAEL]
Not the famous college *chum.*

MICHAEL
[*Takes an ice cube out of his glass, throws it at* HAROLD]
Do a figure eight on that.

HAROLD
Well, well, well. I finally get to meet dear ole Alan after all these years. And in black tie too. Is this my surprise from you, Michael?

LARRY
I think Alan is the one who got the surprise.

DONALD
And, if you'll notice, he's absolutely speechless.

EMORY
I *hope* she's in *shock!* She's a beast!

COWBOY
   [*Indicating* ALAN]
Is it his birthday too?

EMORY
   [*Indicates* COWBOY *to* HAROLD]
That's your surprise.

LARRY
Speaking of beasts.

EMORY
From me to you, darlin'. How do you like it?

HAROLD
Oh, I suppose he has an interesting face and body—but it turns me
right off because he can't talk intelligently about art.

EMORY
Yeah, ain't it a shame.

HAROLD
I could never *love* anyone like that.

EMORY
Never. *Who could?*

HAROLD
I could and *you* could, that's who could! Oh, Mary, she's *gorgeous!*

EMORY
She may be dumb, but she's all yours!

HAROLD
In affairs of the heart, there are no rules! Where'd you ever find
him?

EMORY
Rae knew where.

MICHAEL
   [*To* DONALD]
Rae is Rae Clark. That's R-A-E. She's Emory's dyke friend who
sings at a place in the Village. She wears pinstriped suits and bills
herself "Miss Rae Clark—Songs Tailored to Your Taste."

EMORY
Miss Rae Clark. Songs tailored to your taste!

MICHAEL
Have you ever heard of anything so crummy in your life?

EMORY
Rae's a fabulous chanteuse. I adore the way she does "Down in the
Depths on the Ninetieth Floor."

MICHAEL
The faggot national anthem.
[*Exits to the kitchen singing "Down in the Depths" in a butch bari-
tone*]

HAROLD
[*To EMORY*]
All I can say is thank God for Miss Rae Clark. I think my present
is a super-surprise. I'm so thrilled to get it I'd kiss you, but I don't
want to get blood all over me.

EMORY
Ohhh, look at my sweater!

HAROLD
Wait'll you see your face.

BERNARD
Come on, Emory, let's clean you up. Happy birthday, Harold.

HAROLD
[*Smiles*]
Thanks, love.

EMORY
My sweater is ruined!

MICHAEL
[*From the kitchen*]
Take one of mine in the bedroom.

DONALD
The one on the floor is vicuña.

BERNARD
[*To EMORY*]
You'll feel better after I bathe your face.

64

EMORY
Cheer-up-things-could-get-worse-I-did-and-they-did.
[*BERNARD leads EMORY up the stairs*]

HAROLD
Just another birthday party with the folks.
[*MICHAEL returns with a wine bottle and a green-crystal white-wine glass, pouring en route*]

MICHAEL
Here's a cold bottle of Pouilly-Fuissé I bought especially for you, kiddo.

HAROLD
Pussycat, all is forgiven. You can stay. No. You can stay, but not all is forgiven. Cheers.

MICHAEL
I didn't want it this way, Hallie.

HAROLD
[*Indicating ALAN*]
Who asked Mr. Right to celebrate my birthday?

DONALD
There are no accidents.

HAROLD
[*Referring to DONALD*]
And who asked *him?*

MICHAEL
Guilty again. When I make problems for myself, I go the whole route.

HAROLD
Always got to have your crutch, haven't you?

DONALD
I'm *not* leaving.
[*Goes to the bar, makes himself another martini*]

HAROLD
Nobody ever thinks completely of somebody else. They always please themselves; they always cheat, if only a little bit.

p8.

LARRY
    [*Referring to* ALAN]
Why is he sitting there with his hands over his ears?

DONALD
I think he has an ick.
    [DONALD *looks at* MICHAEL. MICHAEL *returns the look, steely*]

HANK
    [*To* ALAN]
Can I get you a drink?

LARRY
How can he hear you, dummy, with his hands over his ears?

HAROLD
He can hear every word. In fact, he wouldn't miss a word if it killed
him.
    [ALAN *removes his hands from his ears*]
What'd I tell you?

ALAN
I...I...feel sick. I think...I'm going to...throw up.

HAROLD
Say that again and I won't have to take my appetite depressant.
    [ALAN *looks desperately toward* HANK]

HANK
Hang on.
    [HANK *pulls* ALAN's *arm around his neck, lifts him up, takes him up the
stairs*]

HAROLD
Easy does it. One step at a time.
    [BERNARD *and* EMORY *come out of the bath*]

BERNARD
There. Feel better?

EMORY
Oh, Mary, what would I do without you?
    [EMORY *looks at himself in the mirror*]
I am not ready for my close-up, Mr. De Mille. Nor will I be for the
next two weeks.

[*BERNARD picks up* MICHAEL's *sweater off the floor.* HANK *and* ALAN *are midway up the stairs*]

ALAN
I'm going to throw up! Let me go! Let me go!
[*Tears loose of* HANK, *bolts up the remainder of the stairs. He and* EMORY *meet head-on.* EMORY *screams*]

EMORY
Oh, my God, he's after me again!
[EMORY *recoils as* ALAN *whizzes past into the bathroom, slamming the door behind him.* HANK *has reached the bedroom*]

HANK
He's sick.

BERNARD
Yeah, sick in the head. Here, Emory, put this on.

EMORY
Oh, Mary, take me home. My nerves can't stand any more of this tonight.
[EMORY *takes the vicuña sweater from* BERNARD, *starts to put it on. Downstairs,* HAROLD *flamboyantly takes out a cigarette, takes a kitchen match from a striker, steps up on the seat of the couch, and sits on the back of it*]

HAROLD
TURNING ON!
[*With that, he strikes the match on the sole of his shoe and lights up. Through a strained throat*]
Anybody care to join me?
[*Waves the cigarette in a slow pass*]

MICHAEL
Many thanks, no.
[HAROLD *passes it to* LARRY, *who nods negatively*]

DONALD
No, thank you.

HAROLD
[*To* COWBOY]
How about you, Tex?

COWBOY

Yeah.

> [COWBOY *takes the cigarette, makes some audible inhalations through his teeth*]

MICHAEL

I find the sound of the ritual alone utterly humiliating.

> [*Turns away, goes to the bar, makes another drink*]

LARRY

I hate the smell poppers leave on your fingers.

HAROLD

Why don't you get up and wash your hands?

> [EMORY *and* BERNARD *come down the stairs*]

EMORY

Michael, I left the casserole in the oven. You can take it out anytime.

MICHAEL

You're not going.

EMORY

I couldn't eat now anyway.

HAROLD

Well, *I'm* absolutely ravenous. I'm going to eat until I have a fat attack.

MICHAEL

> [*To* EMORY]

I said, you're *not going.*

HAROLD

> [*To* MICHAEL]

Having a cocktail this evening, are we? In my honor?

EMORY

It's your favorite dinner, Hallie. I made it myself.

BERNARD

Who fixed the casserole?

EMORY

Well, *I* made the sauce!

BERNARD
Well, *I* made the salad!

LARRY
Girls, please.

MICHAEL
Please *what!*

HAROLD
Beware the hostile fag. When he's sober, he's dangerous. When he
drinks, he's lethal.

MICHAEL
[*Referring to* HAROLD]
Attention must *not* be paid.

HAROLD
I'm starved, Em, I'm ready for some of your Alice B. Toklas's
opium-baked lasagna.

EMORY
Are you really? Oh, that makes me so pleased, maybe I'll just serve
it before I leave.

MICHAEL
You're not leaving.

BERNARD
I'll help.

LARRY
I better help too. We don't need a nosebleed in the lasagna.

BERNARD
When the sauce is on it, you wouldn't be able to tell the difference
anyway.
[*EMORY, BERNARD, and LARRY exit to the kitchen*]

MICHAEL
[*Proclamation*]
Nobody's going anywhere!

HAROLD
You are going to have schmertz tomorrow you wouldn't believe.

MICHAEL
May I kiss the hem of your schmata, Doctor Freud?

COWBOY
What are you two talking about? I don't understand.

DONALD
He's working through his Oedipus complex, sugar. With a machete.

COWBOY
Huh?
> [*HANK comes down the stairs*]

HANK
Michael, is there any air spray?

HAROLD
Hair spray! You're supposed to be holding his head, not doing his hair.

HANK
Air spray, not *hair* spray.

MICHAEL
There's a can of floral spray right on top of the john.

HANK
Thanks.
> [*HANK goes back upstairs*]

HAROLD
Aren't you going to say "If it was a snake, it would have bitten you"?

MICHAEL
> [*Indicating COWBOY*]
That is something only your friend would say.

HAROLD
> [*To MICHAEL*]
I am turning on and you are just turning.
> [*To DONALD*]
I keep my grass in the medicine cabinet. In a Band-Aid box. Somebody told me it's the safest place. If the cops arrive, you can always lock yourself in the bathroom and flush it down the john.

DONALD
Very cagey.

HAROLD
It makes more sense than where I *was* keeping it—in an oregano jar
in the spice rack. I kept forgetting and accidentally turning my
hateful mother on with the salad.
     [*A beat*]
But I think she liked it. No matter what meal she comes over for—
even if it's breakfast—she says, "Let's have a salad!"

COWBOY
     [*To* MICHAEL]
Why do you say I would say "If it was a snake, it would have bitten
you"? I think that's what I *would* have said.

MICHAEL
Of course you would have, baby. That's the kind of remark your pint-
size brain thinks of. You are definitely the type who still moves his
lips when he reads and who sits in a steam room and says things like
"Hot enough for you?"

COWBOY
I never use the steam room when I go to the gym. It's bad after a
workout. It flattens you down.

MICHAEL
Just after you've broken your back to blow yourself up like a poi-
soned dog.

COWBOY
Yeah.

MICHAEL
You're right, Harold. Not only can he not talk intelligently about art,
he can't even follow from one sentence to the next.

HAROLD
But he's beautiful. He has *unnatural* natural beauty.
     [*Quick palm upheld*]
Not that that means anything.

MICHAEL
It doesn't mean *everything.*

HAROLD
Keep telling yourself that as your hair drops out in handfuls.
[*Quick palm upheld*]
Not that it's not *natural* for one's hair to recede as one reaches seniority. Not that those wonderful lines that have begun creasing our countenances don't make all the difference in the world because they add so much *character.*

MICHAEL
Faggots are worse than women about their age. They think their lives are over at thirty. Physical beauty is not that goddamned important!

HAROLD
Of course not. How could it be—it's only in the eye of the beholder.

MICHAEL
And it's only skin deep—don't forget that one.

HAROLD
Oh, no, I haven't forgotten that one at all. It's only skin-deep and it's *transitory* too. It's *terribly* transitory. I mean, how long does it last—thirty or forty or fifty years at the most—depending on how well you take care of yourself. And not counting, of course, that you might die before it runs out anyway. Yes, it's too bad about this poor boy's face. It's tragic. He's absolutely cursed!
[*Takes COWBOY's face in his hands*]
How can *his* beauty ever compare with *my* soul? And although I have never seen my soul, I understand from my mother's rabbi that it's a knockout. I, however, cannot seem to locate it for a gander. And if I could, I'd sell it in a flash for some skin-deep, transitory, meaningless beauty!
[*ALAN walks weakly into the bedroom and sits on the bed. Downstairs, LARRY enters from the kitchen with salad plates. HANK comes into the bedroom and turns out the lamps. ALAN lies down. Now only the light from the bathroom and the stairwell illuminate the room*]

MICHAEL
[*Makes sign of the cross with his drink in hand*]
Forgive him, Father, for he knows"
not what he do.
[*HANK stands still in the half darkness*]

absurd

72

HAROLD

Michael, you kill me. You don't know what side of the fence you're on. If somebody says something pro-religion, you're against them. If somebody denies God, you're against *them*. One might say that you have some problem in that area. You can't live with it and you can't live without it.

[*EMORY barges through the swinging door, carrying the casserole*]

EMORY

Hot stuff! Comin' through!

MICHAEL
[*To EMORY*]

One could murder you with very little effort.

HAROLD
[*To MICHAEL*]

You hang on to that great insurance policy called The Church.

MICHAEL

That's right. I believe in God, and if it turns out that there really isn't one, OK. Nothing lost. But if it turns out that there *is*—I'm covered.

[*BERNARD enters, carrying a huge salad bowl. He puts it down, lights table candles*]

EMORY
[*To MICHAEL*]

Harriet Hypocrite, that's who you are.

MICHAEL

Right. I'm one of those truly rotten Catholics who gets drunk, sins all night and goes to Mass the next morning.

EMORY

Gilda Guilt. It depends on what you think sin is.

MICHAEL

Would you just shut up your goddamn minty mouth and get back to the goddamn kitchen!

EMORY

Say anything you want—*just don't hit me!*
[*Exits. A beat*]

MICHAEL
Actually, I suppose Emory has a point—I only go to confession
before I get on a plane.

BERNARD
Do you think God's power only exists at thirty thousand feet?

MICHAEL
It must. On the ground, I *am* God. In the air, I'm just one more
scared son of a bitch.
    [*A beat*]

BERNARD
I'm scared on the ground.

COWBOY
Me too.
    [*A beat*]
That is, when I'm not high on pot or up on acid.
    [*HANK comes down the stairs*]

LARRY
    [*To HANK*]
Well, is it bigger than a breadstick?

HANK
    [*Ignores last remark. To MICHAEL*]
He's lying down for a minute.

HAROLD
How does the bathroom smell?

HANK
Better.

MICHAEL
Before it smelled like somebody puked. Now it smells like somebody puked in a gardenia patch.

LARRY
And how does the big hero feel?

HANK
Lay off, will you?
    [*EMORY enters with a basket of napkin-covered rolls, deposits them
    on the table*]

EMORY
Dinner is served!
> [HAROLD *comes to the buffet table*]

HAROLD
Emory, it looks absolutely fabulous.

EMORY
I'd make somebody a good wife.
> [EMORY *serves pasta.* BERNARD *serves the salad, pours wine.*
> MICHAEL *goes to the bar, makes another drink*]

I could cook and do an apartment and entertain...
> [*Grabs a long-stem rose from an arrangement on the table, clenches
> it between his teeth, snaps his fingers and strikes a pose*]

Kiss me quick, I'm Carmen!
> [HAROLD *just looks at him blankly, passes on.* EMORY *takes the
> flower out of his mouth*]

One really needs castanets for that sort of thing.

MICHAEL
And a getaway car.
> [HANK *comes up to the table*]

EMORY
What would you like, big boy?

LARRY
Alan McCarthy, and don't hold the mayo.

EMORY
I can't keep up with you two—
> [*Indicating* HANK, *then* LARRY]

—I thought you were mad at him—now he's bitchin' you. What
gives?

LARRY
Never mind.
> [COWBOY *comes over to the table.* EMORY *gives him a plate of food.*
> BERNARD *gives him salad and a glass of wine.* HANK *moves to the
> couch, sits, and puts his plate and glass on the coffee table.* HAROLD
> *moves to sit on the stairs and eat*]

COWBOY
What is it?

LARRY
Lasagna.

COWBOY
It looks like spaghetti and meatballs sorta flattened out.

DONALD
It's been in the steam room.

COWBOY
It has?

MICHAEL
[*Contemptuously*]
It looks like spaghetti and meatballs sorta flattened out. Ah, yes,
Harold—truly enviable.

HAROLD
As opposed to you, who knows so much about *haute cuisine*.
[*A beat*]
Raconteur, gourmet, troll.
[*LARRY takes a plate of food, goes to sit on the back of the couch from
behind it*]

COWBOY
It's good.

HAROLD
[*Quick*]
You like it, eat it.

MICHAEL
Stuff your mouth so that you can't say anything.
[*DONALD takes a plate*]

HAROLD
Turning.

BERNARD
[*To DONALD*]
Wine?

DONALD
No, thanks.

MICHAEL
Aw, go on, kiddo, force yourself. Have a little *vin ordinaire* to wash down all that depressed pasta.

HAROLD
Sommelier, connoisseur, pig.
> [*DONALD takes the glass of wine, moves up by the bar, puts the glass of wine on it, leans against the wall, eats his food. EMORY hands BERNARD a plate*]

BERNARD
[*To EMORY*]
Aren't you going to have any?

EMORY
No. My lip hurts too much to eat.

MICHAEL
[*Crosses to table, picks up knife*]
I hear if you puts a knife under de bed it cuts de pain.

HAROLD
[*To MICHAEL*]
I hear if you put a knife under your chin it cuts your throat.

EMORY
Anybody going to take a plate up to Alan?

MICHAEL
The punching bag has now dissolved into Flo Nightingale.

LARRY
Hank?

HANK
I don't think he'd have any appetite.
> [*ALAN, as if he's heard his name, gets up from the bed, moves slowly to the top of the stairwell. BERNARD takes his plate, moves near the stairs, sits on the floor. MICHAEL raps the knife on an empty wineglass*]

MICHAEL
Ladies and gentlemen. Correction: Ladies and ladies, I would like to announce that you have just eaten Sebastian Venable.

COWBOY
Just eaten *what?*

MICHAEL
Not *what*, stupid. *Who*. A character in a play. A fairy who was eaten
alive. I mean the chop-chop variety.

COWBOY
Jesus.

HANK
Did Edward Albee write that play?

MICHAEL
No. Tennessee Williams.

HANK
Oh, yeah.

MICHAEL
Albee wrote *Who's Afraid of Virginia Woolf?*

LARRY
Dummy.

HANK
I know that. I just thought maybe he wrote that other one too.

LARRY
Well, you made a mistake.

HANK
So I made a mistake.

LARRY
That's right, you made a mistake.

HANK
What's the difference? You can't add.

COWBOY
Edward who?

MICHAEL
[*To EMORY*]
How much did you pay for him?

EMORY
He was a steal.

78

MICHAEL
He's a ham sandwich—fifty cents anytime of the day or night.

HAROLD
King of the Pig People.
        [*MICHAEL gives him a look. DONALD returns his plate to the table*]

EMORY
        [*To DONALD*]
Would you like some more?

DONALD
No, thank you, Emory. It was very good.

EMORY
Did you like it?

COWBOY
I'm not a steal. I cost twenty dollars.
        [*BERNARD returns his plate*]

EMORY
More?

BERNARD
        [*Nods negatively*]
It was delicious—even if I did make it myself.

EMORY
Isn't anybody having seconds?

HAROLD
I'm having seconds and thirds and maybe even fifths.
        [*Gets up off the stairs, comes toward the table*]
I'm absolutely desperate to keep the weight up.
        [*BERNARD bends to whisper something in EMORY's ear. EMORY nods
        affirmatively and BERNARD crosses to COWBOY and whispers in his
        ear. A beat. COWBOY returns his plate to the buffet and follows
        EMORY and BERNARD into the kitchen*]

MICHAEL
        [*Parodying HAROLD*]
You're *absolutely* paranoid about *absolutely* everything.

HAROLD
Oh, yeah, well, why don't you *not* tell me about it.

MICHAEL
You starve yourself all day, living on coffee and cottage cheese so that you can gorge yourself at one meal. Then you feel guilty and moan and groan about how fat you are and how ugly you are when the truth is you're no fatter or thinner than you ever are.

EMORY
Polly Paranoia.
[*EMORY moves to the coffee table to take* HANK'*s empty plate*]

HANK
Just great, Emory.

EMORY
Connie Casserole, no-trouble-at-all-oh-Mary, D.A.

MICHAEL
[*To* HAROLD]
...And this pathological lateness. It's downright *crazy*.

HAROLD
Turning.

MICHAEL
Standing before a bathroom mirror for hours and hours before you can walk out on the street. And looking no different after Christ knows how many applications of Christ knows how many ointments and salves and creams and masks.

HAROLD
I've got bad skin, what can I tell you.

MICHAEL
Who wouldn't after they deliberately take a pair of tweezers and *deliberately* mutilate their pores—no wonder you've got holes in your face after the hack job you've done on yourself year in and year out!

HAROLD
[*Coolly but definitely*]
You hateful sow.

MICHAEL
Yes, you've got scars on your face—but they're not that bad and if you'd leave yourself alone you wouldn't have any more than you've already awarded yourself.

HAROLD

You'd really like me to compliment you now for being so honest,
wouldn't you? For being my best friend who will tell me what even
my best friends won't tell me. Swine.

MICHAEL

And the pills!
        [*Announcement to group*]
Harold has been gathering, saving, and storing up barbiturates for the
last year like a goddamn squirrel. Hundreds of Nembutals, hundreds of
Seconals. All in preparation for and anticipation of the long winter of
his death.
        [*Silence*]
But I tell you right now, Hallie. When the time comes, you'll never
have the guts. It's not always like it happens in plays, not all faggots
bump themselves off at the end of the story.

HAROLD

What you say may be true. Time will undoubtedly tell. But, in the
meantime, you've left out one detail—the cosmetics and astringents
are *paid* for, the bathroom is *paid* for, the tweezers are *paid* for, and
the pills *are paid for!*
        [*EMORY darts in and over to the light switch, plunges the room into
        darkness except for the light from the tapers on the buffet table, and
        begins to sing "Happy Birthday." Immediately* BERNARD *pushes the
        swinging door open and* COWBOY *enters carrying a cake ablaze with
        candles. Everyone has now joined in with "Happy birthday, dear
        HAROLD, happy birthday to you." This is followed by a round of
        applause.* MICHAEL *turns, goes to the bar, makes another drink*]

EMORY

Blow out your candles, Mary, and make a wish!

MICHAEL

        [*To himself*]
Blow out your candles, *Laura.*
        [*COWBOY has brought cake over in front of* HAROLD. *He thinks a
        minute, blows out the candles. More applause*]

EMORY

Awwww, she's thirty-two years young!

HAROLD

        [*Groans, holds his head*]
Ohh, my God!

[*BERNARD has brought in cake plates and forks. The room remains lit only by candlelight from the buffet table.* COWBOY *returns the cake to the table and* BERNARD *begins to cut it and put the pieces on the plates*]

HANK
Now you have to open your gifts.

HAROLD
Do I have to open them here?

EMORY
Of course you've got to open them here.
[*Hands* HAROLD *a gift.* HAROLD *begins to rip the paper off*]

HAROLD
Where's the card?

EMORY
Here.

HAROLD
Oh. From Larry.
[*Finishes tearing off the paper*]
It's *heaven!* Oh, I just love it, Larry.
[HAROLD *holds up a graphic design—a large-scale deed to Boardwalk, like those used in a Monopoly game*]

COWBOY
What is it?

HAROLD
It's the deed to Boardwalk.

EMORY
Oh, gay pop art!

DONALD
[*To* LARRY]
It's sensational. Did you do it?

LARRY
Yes.

HAROLD
Oh, it's super, Larry. It goes up the minute I get home.
[HAROLD *gives* LARRY *a peck on the cheek*]

COWBOY
[*To* HAROLD]
I don't get it—you cruise Atlantic City or something?

MICHAEL
Will somebody get him out of here!
[HAROLD *has torn open another gift, takes the card from inside*]

HAROLD
Oh, what a nifty sweater! Thank you, Hank.

HANK
You can take it back and pick out another one if you want to.

HAROLD
I think this one is just nifty.
[DONALD *goes to the bar, makes himself a brandy and soda*]

BERNARD
Who wants cake?

EMORY
Everybody?

DONALD
None for me.

MICHAEL
I'd just like to sleep on mine, thank you.
[HANK *comes over to the table.* BERNARD *gives him a plate of cake, passes another one to* COWBOY *and a third to* LARRY. HAROLD *has torn the paper off another gift. Suddenly laughs aloud*]

HAROLD
Oh, Bernard! How divine! Look, everybody! Bejeweled knee pads!
[*Holds up a pair of basketball knee pads with sequin initials*]

BERNARD
Monogrammed!

EMORY
Bernard, you're a camp!

MICHAEL
Y'all heard of Gloria DeHaven and Billy De Wolfe, well, dis here is Rosemary De Camp!

BERNARD
Who?

EMORY
I never miss a Rosemary De Camp picture.

HANK
I've never heard of her.

COWBOY
Me neither.

HANK
Not all of us spent their childhood in a movie house, Michael. Some of us played baseball.

DONALD
And mowed the lawn.

EMORY
Well, *I* know who Rosemary De Camp is.

MICHAEL
You would. It's a cinch you wouldn't recognize a baseball or a lawn mower.
        [*HAROLD has unwrapped his last gift. He is silent. Pause*]

HAROLD
Thank you, Michael.

MICHAEL
What?
        [*Turns to see the gift*]
Oh.
        [*A beat*]
You're welcome.
        [*MICHAEL finishes off his drink, returns to the bar*]

LARRY
What is it, Harold?
        [*A beat*]

HAROLD
It's a photograph of him in a silver frame. And there's an inscription engraved and the date.

BERNARD
What's it say?

HAROLD
Just...something personal.
  [*MICHAEL spins round from the bar*]

MICHAEL
Hey, Bernard, what do you say we have a little music to liven things up!

BERNARD
OK.

EMORY
Yeah, I feel like dancing.

MICHAEL
How about something good and ethnic, Emory—one of your specialties, like a military toe tap with sparklers.

EMORY
I don't do that at birthdays—only on the Fourth of July.
  [*BERNARD puts on a romantic record. EMORY goes to BERNARD.
  They start to dance slowly*]

LARRY
Come on, Michael.

MICHAEL
I only lead.

LARRY
I can follow.
  [*They start to dance*]

HAROLD
Come on, Tex, you're on.
  [*COWBOY gets to his feet but is a washout as a dancing partner.
  HAROLD gives up, takes out another cigarette, strikes a match. As he
  does, he catches sight of someone over by the stairs, walks over to
  ALAN. Blows out match*]
Wanna dance?

EMORY
  [*Sees ALAN*]
Uh-oh. Yvonne the Terrible is back.

MICHAEL

Oh, hello, Alan. Feel better? This is where you came in, isn't it?
  [ALAN *starts to cross directly to the door.* MICHAEL *breaks away*]
Excuse me, Larry...
  [ALAN *has reached the door and has started to open it as* MICHAEL
  intercepts, slams the door with one hand, and leans against it,
  crossing his legs]
As they say in the Deep South, don't rush off in the heat of the day.

HAROLD

Revolution complete.
  [MICHAEL *slowly takes* ALAN *by the arm, walks him slowly back into*
  the room]

MICHAEL

...You missed the cake—and you missed the opening of the gifts—
but you're still in luck. You're just in time for a party game.
  [*They have reached the phonograph.* MICHAEL *rejects the record. The*
  music stops, the dancing stops. MICHAEL *releases* ALAN, *claps his*
  hands]
...Hey, everybody! Game time!
  [ALAN *starts to move.* MICHAEL *catches him gently by the sleeve*]

HAROLD

Why don't you just let him go, Michael?

MICHAEL

He can go if he wants to—but not before we play a little game.

EMORY

What's it going to be—movie-star gin?

MICHAEL

That's too faggy for Alan to play—he wouldn't be any good at it.

BERNARD

What about Likes and Dislikes?
  [MICHAEL *lets go of* ALAN, *takes a pencil and pad from the desk*]

MICHAEL

It's too much trouble to find enough pencils, and besides, Emory
always puts down the same thing. He dislikes artificial fruit and
flowers and coffee grinders made into lamps—and he likes Mabel
Mercer, poodles, and *All About Eve*—the screenplay of which he will
then recite *verbatim*.

EMORY
I put down other things sometimes.

MICHAEL
Like a tan out of season?

EMORY
I just always put down little "Chi-Chi" because I adore her so much.

MICHAEL
If one is of the masculine gender, a poodle is the *insignia* of one's deviation.

BERNARD
You know why old ladies like poodles—because they go down on them.

EMORY
They do not!

LARRY
We could play B for Botticelli.

MICHAEL
We *could* play *Spin* the Botticelli, but we're not going to.
[*A beat*]

HAROLD
What would you like to play, Michael—the Truth Game?
[*MICHAEL chuckles to himself*]

MICHAEL
Cute, Hallie.

HAROLD
Or do you want to play Murder? You all remember that one, don't you?

MICHAEL
[*To HAROLD*]
Very, very cute.

DONALD
As I recall, they're quite similar. The rules are the same in both— you kill somebody.

MICHAEL
In affairs of the heart, there are no rules. Isn't that right, Harold?

HAROLD
That's what I always say.

MICHAEL
Well, that's the name of the game. The Affairs of the Heart.

COWBOY
I've never heard of that one.

MICHAEL
Of course you've never heard of it—I just made it up, baby doll.
Affairs of the Heart is a combination of both the Truth Game and
Murder—with a new twist.

HAROLD
I can hardly wait to find out what that is.

ALAN
Mickey, I'm leaving.
      [*Starts to move*]

MICHAEL
      [*Firmly, flatly*]
Stay where you are.

HAROLD
Michael, let him go.

MICHAEL
He really doesn't *want* to. If he did, he'd have left a long time ago—
or he wouldn't have come here in the first place.

ALAN
      [*Holding his forehead*]
...Mickey, I don't *feel* well!

MICHAEL
      [*Low tone, but distinctly articulate*]
My name is Michael. I am called Michael. You must never call anyone called Michael Mickey. Those of us who are named Michael are
very nervous about it. If you don't believe it—try it.

ALAN
I'm sorry. I can't think.

MICHAEL

You can think. What you can't do—is leave. It's like watching an
accident on the highway—you can't look at it and you can't look
away.

ALAN

I...feel...weak...

MICHAEL

You are weak. Much weaker than I think you realize.
[*Takes* ALAN *by the arm, leads him to a chair. Slowly, deliberately,
pushes him down into it*]
Now! Who's going to play with Alan and me? Everyone?

HAROLD

I have no intention of playing.

DONALD

Nor do I.

MICHAEL

Well, not everyone is a participant in *life*. There are always those
who stand on the sidelines and watch.

LARRY

What's the game?

MICHAEL

Simply this: We all have to call on the telephone the *one person* we
truly believe we have loved.

HANK

I'm not playing.

LARRY

Oh, yes, you are.

HANK

You'd like for me to play, wouldn't you?

LARRY

You bet I would. I'd like to know who you'd call after all the
fancy speeches I've heard lately. Who would you call? Would you
call me?

MICHAEL
[*To* BERNARD]
Sounds like there's, how you say, trouble in paradise.

HAROLD
If there isn't, I think you'll be able to stir up some.

HANK
And who would *you* call? Don't think I think for one minute it would be me. Or that one call would do it. You'd have to make several, wouldn't you? About three long-distance and God only knows how many locals.

COWBOY
I'm glad I don't have to pay the bill.

MICHAEL
Quiet!

HAROLD
[*Loud whisper to* COWBOY]
Oh, don't worry, Michael won't pay it either.

MICHAEL
Now, here's how it works.

LARRY
I thought you said there were no rules.

MICHAEL
That's right. In Affairs of the Heart, there are no rules. This is the goddamn point system!
[*No response from anyone. A beat*]
If you make the call, you get one point. If the person you are calling answers, you get two more points. If somebody else answers, you get only one. If there's no answer at all, you're screwed.

DONALD
You're screwed if you make the call.

HAROLD
You're a *fool*—if you screw yourself.

MICHAEL
When you get the person whom you are calling on the line—if you tell them who you are, you get two points. And then—if you tell them that you *love* them—you get a bonus of five more points!

90

HAROLD
Hateful.

MICHAEL
Therefore you can get as many as ten points and as few as one.

HAROLD
You can get as few as none—if you know how to work it.

MICHAEL
The one with the highest score wins.

ALAN
Hank. Let's get out of here.

EMORY
Well, now. Did you hear that!

MICHAEL
Just the two of you together. The pals...the guys...the buddy-buddies...the he-men.

EMORY
I think Larry might have something to say about that.

BERNARD
Emory.

MICHAEL
The duenna speaks.
        [*Crosses to take the telephone from the desk, brings it to the group*]
So who's playing? Not including Cowboy, who, as a gift, is neuter.
And, of course, le voyeur.
        [*A beat*]
Emory? Bernard?

BERNARD
I don't think I want to play.

MICHAEL
Why, Bernard! Where's your fun-loving spirit?

BERNARD
I don't think this game is fun.

HAROLD
It's absolutely hateful.

ALAN
Hank, leave with me.

HANK
You don't understand, Alan. I can't. You can…but I can't.

ALAN
Why, Hank? Why can't you?

LARRY
        [*To* HANK]
If he doesn't understand, why don't you explain it to him?

MICHAEL
I'll explain it.

HAROLD
I had a feeling you might.

MICHAEL
Although I doubt that it'll make any difference. That type refuses to
understand that which they do not wish to accept. They reject certain
facts. And Alan is decidedly from The Ostrich School of Reality.
        [*A beat*]
Alan…Larry and Hank are lovers. Not just roommates, *bed*mates.
Lovers.

ALAN
Michael!

MICHAEL
No man's still got a *roommate* when he's over thirty years old. If
they're not lovers, they're sisters.

LARRY
Hank is the one who's over thirty.

MICHAEL
Well, you're pushing it!

ALAN
…Hank?
        [*A beat*]

HANK
Yes, Alan. Larry is my lover.

ALAN
But...but...you're married.
[MICHAEL, LARRY, EMORY, and COWBOY are sent into instant gales of laughter]

HAROLD
I think you said the wrong thing.

MICHAEL
Don't you love that quaint little idea—if a man is married, then he is automatically heterosexual.
[A beat]
Alan—Hank swings both ways—with a definite preference.
[A beat]
Now. Who makes the first call? Emory?

EMORY
You go, Bernard.

BERNARD
I don't want to.

EMORY
I don't want to either. I don't want to at all.

DONALD
[To himself]
There are no accidents.

MICHAEL
Then, may I say, on your way home I hope you *will* yourself over an embankment.

EMORY
[To BERNARD]
Go on. Call up Peter Dahlbeck. That's who you'd like to call, isn't it?

MICHAEL
Who is Peter Dahlbeck?

EMORY
The boy in Detroit whose family Bernard's mother has been a laundress for since he was a pickaninny.

BERNARD
I worked for them too—after school and every summer.

EMORY
It's always been a large order of Hero Worship.

BERNARD
I think I've loved him all my life. But he never knew I was alive.
Besides, he's straight.

COWBOY
So nothing ever happened between you?

EMORY
Oh, they finally made it—in the pool house one night after a drunk-
en swimming party.

LARRY
With the right wine and the right music there're damn few that
aren't curious.

MICHAEL
Sounds like there's a lot of Lady Chatterley in Mr. Dahlbeck,
wouldn't you say, Donald?

DONALD
I've never been an O'Hara fan myself.

BERNARD
…And afterwards we went swimming in the nude in the dark with
only the moon reflecting on the water.

DONALD
Nor Thomas Merton.

BERNARD
It was beautiful.

MICHAEL
How romantic. And then the next morning you took him his coffee
and Alka-Seltzer on a tray.

BERNARD
It was in the afternoon. I remember I was worried sick all morning
about having to face him. But he pretended like nothing at all had
happened.

MICHAEL
Christ, he must have been so drunk he didn't remember a thing.

BERNARD
Yeah. I was sure relieved.

MICHAEL
Odd how that works. And now, for ten points, get that liar on the phone.
[*A beat.* BERNARD *picks up the phone, dials*]

LARRY
You *know* the number?

BERNARD
Sure. He's back in Grosse Pointe, living at home. He just got separated from his third wife.
[*All watch* BERNARD *as he puts the receiver to his ear, waits. A beat. He hangs up quickly*]

EMORY
D.A. or B.Y.?

MICHAEL
He didn't even give it time to find out.
[*Coaxing*]
Go ahead, Bernard. Pick up the phone and dial. You'll think of something. You know you want to call him. You know that, don't you? Well, go ahead. Your curiosity has got the best of you now. So...go on, call him.
[*A beat.* BERNARD *picks up the receiver, dials again. Lets it ring this time*]

HAROLD
Hateful.

COWBOY
What's D.A. or B.Y.?

EMORY
That's operator lingo. It means—"Doesn't Answer" or "Busy."

BERNARD
...Hello?

MICHAEL
One point.
[*Efficiently takes note on the pad*]

BERNARD
Who's speaking? Oh…Mrs. Dahlbeck.

MICHAEL
       [*Taking note*]
One point.

BERNARD
…It's Bernard—Francine's boy.

EMORY
Son, not *boy.*

BERNARD
…How are you? Good. Good. Oh, just fine, thank you. Mrs.
Dahlbeck…is… Peter…at home? Oh. Oh, I see.

MICHAEL
       [*Shakes his head*]
Shhhhiiii…

BERNARD
…Oh, no. No, it's nothing important. I just wanted to…to tell
him…that…to tell him I…I…

MICHAEL
       [*Prompting flatly*]
I love him. That I've always loved him.

BERNARD
…that I was sorry to hear about him and his wife.

MICHAEL
No points!

BERNARD
…My mother wrote me. Yes. It is. It really is. Well. Would you just
tell him I called and said…that I was…just…very, very sorry to hear
and I…hope… they can get everything straightened out. Yes. Yes.
Well, good night. Goodbye.
       [*Hangs up slowly.* MICHAEL *draws a definite line across his pad,
       makes a definite period*]

MICHAEL
Two points total. Terrible. Next!
       [MICHAEL *whisks the phone out of* BERNARD's *hands, gives it to*
       EMORY]

96

EMORY
Are you all right, Bernard?

BERNARD
   [*Almost to himself*]
Why did I call? Why did I do that?

LARRY
   [*To* BERNARD]
Where was he?

BERNARD
Out on a date.

MICHAEL
Come on, Emory. Punch in.
   [EMORY *picks up the phone, dials information. A beat*]

EMORY
Could I have the number, please—in the Bronx—for a Delbert
Botts.

LARRY
A Delbert Botts! How many can there be!

BERNARD
Oh, I wish I hadn't called now.

EMORY
...No, the residence number, please.
   [*Waves his hand at* MICHAEL, *signaling for the pencil.* MICHAEL
   hands it to him. He writes on the white plastic phone case]
...Thank you.
   [*A beat. And he indignantly slams down the receiver*]
I do wish information would stop calling me "Ma'am"!

MICHAEL
By all means, scribble all over the telephone.
   [*Snatches the pencil from* EMORY's *hands*]

EMORY
It comes off with a little spit.

MICHAEL
Like a lot of things.

LARRY
Who the hell is Delbert Botts?

EMORY
The one person I have always loved.
[*To* MICHAEL]
That's who you said call, isn't it?

MICHAEL
That's right, Emory Board.

LARRY
How could you love anybody with a name like that?

MICHAEL
Yes, Emory, you couldn't love anybody with a name like that. It
wouldn't look good on a place card. Isn't that right, Alan?
[MICHAEL *slaps* ALAN *on the shoulder.* ALAN *is silent.* MICHAEL
snickers]

EMORY
I admit his name is not so good—but he is absolutely beautiful. At
least, he was when I was in high school. Of course, I haven't seen
him since and he was about seven years older than I even then.

MICHAEL
Christ, you better call him quick before he dies.

EMORY
I've loved him ever since the first day I laid eyes on him, which was
when I was in the fifth grade and he was a senior. Then, he went
away to college and by the time he got out *I* was in high school, and
he had become a dentist.

MICHAEL
[*With incredulous disgust*]
A dentist!

EMORY
Yes. Delbert Botts, D.D.S. And he opened his office in a bank
building.

HAROLD
And you went and had every tooth in your head pulled out, right?

EMORY
No. I just had my teeth cleaned, that's all.
            [DONALD *turns from the bar with two drinks in his hands*]

BERNARD
            [*To himself*]
Oh, I shouldn't have called.

MICHAEL
Will you shut up, Bernard! And take your boring, sleep-making icks
somewhere else. *Go!*
            [MICHAEL *extends a pointed finger toward the steps.* BERNARD *takes*
            the wine bottle and his glass and moves toward the stairs, pouring
            himself another drink on the way]

EMORY
I remember I looked right into his eyes the whole time and I kept
wanting to bite his fingers.

HAROLD
Well, it's absolutely mind-boggling.

MICHAEL
Phyllis Phallic.

HAROLD
It absolutely boggles the mind.
            [DONALD *brings one of the drinks to* ALAN. ALAN *takes it, drinks it*
            down]

MICHAEL
            [*Referring to* DONALD]
Sara Samaritan.

EMORY
…I told him I was having my teeth cleaned for the Junior-Senior Prom,
for which I was in charge of decorations. I told him it was a celestial
theme and I was cutting stars out of tinfoil and making clouds out of
chicken wire and angel's hair.
            [*A beat*]
He couldn't have been less impressed.

COWBOY
I got angel's hair down my shirt once at Christmastime. Gosh, did it
itch!

EMORY
…I told him I was going to burn incense in pots so that white fog would hover over the dance floor and it would look like heaven—just like I'd seen it in a Rita Hayworth movie. I can't remember the title.

MICHAEL
The picture was called *Down to Earth*. Any *kid* knows that.

COWBOY
…And it made little tiny cuts in the creases of my fingers. Man, did they sting! It would be terrible if you got that stuff in your…
[*MICHAEL circles slowly toward him*]
I'll be quiet.

EMORY
He was engaged to this stupid-ass girl named Loraine whose mother was truly Supercunt.

MICHAEL
Don't digress.

EMORY
Well, anyway, I was a wreck. I mean a total mess. I couldn't eat, sleep, stand up, sit down, *nothing*. I could hardly cut out silver stars or finish the clouds for the prom. So I called him on the telephone and asked if I could see him alone.

HAROLD
Clearly not the coolest of moves.
[*DONALD looks at ALAN. ALAN looks away*]

EMORY
He said OK and told me to come by his house. I was so nervous my hands were shaking and my voice was unsteady. I couldn't look at him this time—I just stared straight in space and blurted out why I'd come. I told him…I wanted him to be my friend. I said that I had never had a friend who I could talk to and tell everything and trust. I asked him if he would be my friend.

COWBOY
You poor bastard.

MICHAEL
SHHHHHH!

100

BERNARD
What'd he say?

EMORY
He said he would be glad to be my friend. And anytime I ever
wanted to see him or call him—to just call him and he'd see me.
And he shook my trembling wet hand and I left on a cloud.

MICHAEL
One of the ones you made yourself.

EMORY
And the next day I went and bought him a gold-plated cigarette
lighter and had his initials monogrammed on it and wrote a card
that said "From your friend, Emory."

HAROLD
Seventeen years old and already big with the gifts.

COWBOY
Yeah. And cards too.

EMORY
...And then the night of the prom I found out.

BERNARD
Found out what?

EMORY
I heard two girls I knew giggling together. They were standing
behind some goddamn corrugated-cardboard Greek columns I had
borrowed from a department store and had draped with yards and
yards of goddamn cheesecloth. Oh, Mary, it takes a fairy to make
something pretty.

MICHAEL
Don't digress.

EMORY
This girl who was telling the story said she had heard it from her
mother—and her mother had heard it from Loraine's mother.
[*To MICHAEL*]
You see, Loraine and her mother were not beside the point.
[*Back to the group*]
Obviously, Del had told Loraine about my calling and about the
gift.
[*A beat*]

EMORY [*Cont'd*]
Pretty soon everybody at the dance had heard about it and they
were laughing and making jokes. Everybody knew I had a crush
on Doctor Delbert Botts and that I had asked him to be my
friend.
[*A beat*]
What they didn't know was that I *loved* him. And that I would go on
loving him years after they had all forgotten my funny secret.
[*Pause*]

HAROLD
Well, I for one need an insulin injection.

MICHAEL
Call him.

BERNARD
Don't, Emory.

MICHAEL
Since when are you telling him what to do!

EMORY
[*To* BERNARD]
What do I care—I'm pissed! I'll do anything. Three times.

BERNARD
Don't. *Please!*

MICHAEL
I said call him.

BERNARD
Don't! You'll be sorry. Take my word for it.

EMORY
What have I got to lose?

BERNARD
Your dignity. That's what you've got to lose.

MICHAEL
Well, *that's* a knee-slapper! I love *your* telling *him* about dignity
when you allow him to degrade you constantly by Uncle Tom–ing
you to death.

BERNARD
He can do it, Michael. *I* can do it. But *you can't* do it.

MICHAEL
Isn't that discrimination?

BERNARD
I don't like it from him and I don't like it from me—but I do it to myself and I let him do it. I let him do it because it's the only thing that, to him, makes him my equal. We both got the short end of the stick—but I got a hell of a lot more than he did and he knows it. I let him Uncle Tom me just so he can tell himself he's not a complete loser.

MICHAEL
How very considerate.

BERNARD
It's his defense. You have your defense, Michael. But it's indescribable.
[*EMORY quietly licks his finger and begins to rub the number off the telephone case*]

MICHAEL
[*To* BERNARD]
Y'all want to hear a little polite parlor jest from the liberal Deep South? Do you know why *Nigras* have such big lips? Because they're always going "P-p-p-p-a-a-a-h!"
[*The labial noise is exasperating with lazy disgust as he shuffles about the room*]

DONALD
Christ, Michael!

MICHAEL
[*Unsuccessfully tries to tear the phone away from* EMORY]
I can do without your goddamn spit all over my telephone, you nellie coward.

EMORY
I may be nellie, but I'm no coward.
[*Starts to dial*]
Bernard, forgive me. I'm sorry. I won't ever say those things to you again.
[*MICHAEL watches triumphant.* BERNARD *pours another glass of wine. A beat*]
B.Y.

MICHAEL
It's busy?

EMORY
[Nods]
Loraine is probably talking to her mother. Oh, yes. Delbert married
Loraine.

MICHAEL
I'm sorry, you'll have to forfeit your turn. We can't wait.
[Takes the phone, hands it to LARRY, who starts to dial]

HAROLD
[To LARRY]
Well, you're not wasting any time.

HANK
Who are you calling?

LARRY
Charlie.
[EMORY gets up, jerks the phone out of LARRY's hands]

EMORY
I refuse to forfeit my turn! It's *my turn*, and I'm taking it!

MICHAEL
That's the spirit, Emory! *Hit that iceberg—don't miss it! Hit it!
Goddamn it!* I want a smash of a finale!

EMORY
Oh, God, I'm drunk.

MICHAEL
A falling-down-drunk-nellie-queen.

HAROLD
Well, that's the pot calling the kettle beige!

MICHAEL
[Snapping. To HAROLD]
I am not drunk! You cannot tell that I am drunk! Donald! I'm not
drunk! Am I!

DONALD
I'm drunk.

104

EMORY
So am I. I am a *major drunk*.

MICHAEL
[*To* EMORY]
Shut up and dial!

EMORY
[*Dialing*]
I am a major drunk of this or any other season.

DONALD
[*To* MICHAEL]
Don't you mean 'shut up and deal'?

EMORY
...It's ringing. It is no longer B.Y. Hello?

MICHAEL
[*Taking note*]
One point.

EMORY
...Who's speaking? Who?... Doctor Delbert Botts?

MICHAEL
Two points.

EMORY
Oh, Del, is this really you? Oh, nobody. You don't know me. You
wouldn't remember me. I'm...just a friend. A falling-down drunken
friend. Hello? Hello? Hello?
[*Lowers the receiver*]
He hung up.
[EMORY *hangs up the telephone*]

MICHAEL
Three points total. You're winning.

EMORY
He said I must have the wrong party.
[BERNARD *gets up, goes into the kitchen*]

HAROLD
He's right. We have the wrong party. We should be somewhere
else.

EMORY
It's your party, Hallie. Aren't you having a good time?

HAROLD
Simply fabulous. And what about you? Are you having a good time,
Emory? Are you having as good a time as you thought you would?
    [*LARRY takes the phone*]

MICHAEL
If you're bored, Harold, we could sing "Happy Birthday" again—to
the tune of "Havah Nageelah."
    [*HAROLD takes out another cigarette*]

HAROLD
Not for all the tea in Mexico.
    [*Lights up*]

HANK
My turn now.

LARRY
It's my turn to call Charlie.

HANK
No. Let me.

LARRY
Are *you* going to call Charlie?

MICHAEL
The score is three to two. Emory's favor.

ALAN
Don't, Hank. Don't you see—Bernard was right.

HANK
    [*Firmly, to ALAN*]
I want to.
    [*A beat. Holds out his hand for the phone*]
Larry?
    [*A beat*]

LARRY
    [*Gives him the phone*]
Be my eager guest.

106

COWBOY
[*To* LARRY]
Is he going to call Charlie for you?
[LARRY *breaks into laughter.* HANK *starts to dial*]

LARRY
Charlie is all the people I cheat on Hank with.

DONALD
With whom I cheat on Hank.

MICHAEL
The butcher, the baker, the candlestick maker.

LARRY
Right! I love 'em all. And what he refuses to understand—is that I've got to *have* 'em all. I am *not* the marrying kind, and I never will be.

HAROLD
Gypsy feet.

LARRY
Who are you calling?

MICHAEL
Jealous?

LARRY
Curious as hell!

MICHAEL
And a little jealous too.

LARRY
Who are you calling?

MICHAEL
Did it ever occur to you that Hank might be doing the same thing behind your back that you do behind his?

LARRY
I wish to Christ he would. It'd make life a hell of a lot easier. Who are you calling?

HAROLD
Whoever it is, they're not sitting on top of the telephone.

HANK
Hello?

COWBOY
They must have been in the tub.

MICHAEL
[*Snaps at COWBOY*]
Eighty-six!
[*COWBOY goes over to a far corner, sits down. BERNARD enters,
uncorking another bottle of wine. Taking note*]
One point.

HANK
…I'd like to leave a message.

MICHAEL
Not in. One point.

HANK
Would you say that Hank called? Yes, it is. Oh, good evening. How
are you?

LARRY
Who the hell *is* that?

HANK
Yes, that's right—the message is for my roommate, Larry. Just say
that I called and…

LARRY
It's our answering service!

HANK
…and said…I love you.

MICHAEL
Five points! You said it! You get five goddamn points for saying it!

ALAN
Hank! Hank!… Are you crazy?

HANK
…No. You didn't hear me incorrectly. That's what I said. The mes-
sage is for Larry and it's from me, Hank, and it is just as I said:
I…love…you. Thanks. [*Hangs up*]

108

MICHAEL
Seven points total! Hank, you're ahead, baby. You're way, way ahead of everybody!

ALAN
Why?... Oh, Hank, why? Why did you do that?

HANK
Because I do love him. And I don't care who knows it.

ALAN
Don't say that.

HANK
Why not? It's the truth.

ALAN
I can't believe you.

HANK
[*Directly to* ALAN]
I left my wife and family for Larry.

ALAN
I'm really not interested in hearing about it.

MICHAEL
Sure you are. Go ahead, Hankola, tell him all about it.

ALAN
No! I don't want to hear it. It's disgusting!
[*A beat*]

HANK
Some men do it for another woman.

ALAN
Well, I could understand *that*. That's *normal*.

HANK
It just doesn't always work out that way, Alan. No matter how you might want it to. And God knows, nobody ever wanted it more than I did. I really and truly felt that I was in love with my wife when I married her. It wasn't altogether my trying to prove something to myself. I did love her and she loved me. But...there was always that something there...

DONALD
You mean your attraction to your own sex.

HANK
Yes.

ALAN
Always?

HANK
I don't know. I suppose so.

EMORY
I've known what I was since I was four years old.

MICHAEL
Everybody's always known it about *you*, Emory.

DONALD
I've always known it about myself too.

HANK
I don't know when it was that I started admitting it to myself. For so long I either labeled it something else or denied it completely.

MICHAEL
Christ-was-I-drunk-last-night.

HANK
And then there came a time when I just couldn't lie to myself any-more... I thought about it but I never did anything about it. I think the first time was during my wife's last pregnancy. We lived near New Haven—in the country. She and the kids still live there. Well, anyway, there was a teachers' meeting here in New York. She didn't feel up to the trip and I came alone. And that day on the train I began to think about it and think about it and think about it. I thought of nothing else the whole trip. And within fif-teen minutes after I had arrived I had picked up a guy in the men's room of Grand Central Station.

ALAN
    [*Quietly*]
Jesus.

110

HANK

I'd never done anything like that in my life before and I was
scared to death. But he turned out to be a nice fellow. I've never
seen him again and it's funny I can't even remember his name
anymore.
      [A *beat*]
Anyway. After that, it got easier.

HAROLD

Practice makes perfect.

HANK

And then...sometime later...not very long after, Larry was in New
Haven and we met at a party my wife and I had gone in town for.

EMORY

And your real troubles began.

HANK

That was two years ago.

LARRY

Why am I always the goddamn villain in the piece! If I'm not
thought of as a happy-home wrecker, I'm an impossible son of a
bitch to live with!

HAROLD

Guilt turns to hostility. Isn't that right, Michael?

MICHAEL

Go stick your tweezers in your cheek.

LARRY

I'm fed up to the teeth with everybody feeling so goddamn sorry
for poor shat-upon Hank.

EMORY

Aw, Larry, everybody knows you're Frieda Fickle.

LARRY

I've never made any promises and I never intend to. It's my right to
lead my sex life without answering to *anybody*—Hank included!
And if those terms are not acceptable, then we must not live together.
Numerous relations is a part of the way I am!

EMORY

You don't have to be gay to be a wanton.

LARRY
By the way I am, I don't mean being gay—I mean my sexual
appetite. And I don't think of myself as a wanton. Emory, you are
the most promiscuous person I know.

EMORY
I am not promiscuous at all!

MICHAEL
Not by choice. By design. Why would anybody want to go to bed
with a flaming little sissy like you?

BERNARD
Michael!

MICHAEL
[*To EMORY*]
Who'd make a pass at you—I'll tell you who—nobody. Except
maybe some fugitive from the Braille Institute.

BERNARD
[*To EMORY*]
Why do you let him talk to you that way?

HAROLD
Physical beauty is not everything.

MICHAEL
Thank you, Quasimodo.

LARRY
What do you think it's like living with the goddamn gestapo! I can't
breathe without getting the third degree!

MICHAEL
Larry, it's your turn to call.

LARRY
I can't take all that let's-be-faithful-and-never-look-at-another-
person routine. It just doesn't work. If you want to promise
that, fine. Then do it and stick to it. But if you *have* to promise
it—as far as I'm concerned—nothing finishes a relationship
faster.

HAROLD
Give me Librium or give me Meth.

BERNARD
[*Intoxicated now*]
Yeah, freedom, baby! Freedom!

LARRY
You gotta have it! It can't work any other way. And the ones who swear their undying fidelity are lying. Most of them, anyway—ninety percent of them. They cheat on each other constantly and lie through their teeth. I'm sorry, I can't be like that and it drives Hank up the wall.

HANK
There is that ten percent.

LARRY
The only way it stands a chance is with some sort of an understanding.

HANK
I've tried to go along with that.

LARRY
Aw, *come on!*

HANK
I agreed to an agreement.

LARRY
Your agreement.

MICHAEL
What agreement?

LARRY
A ménage.

HAROLD
The lover's agreement.

LARRY
Look, I know a lot of people think it's the answer. They don't consider it cheating. But it's not my style.

HANK
Well, *I* certainly didn't want it.

LARRY
Then who suggested it?

HANK
It was a compromise.

LARRY
Exactly.

HANK
And you agreed.

LARRY
I didn't agree to anything. You agreed to your own proposal and *informed me* that I agreed.

COWBOY
I don't understand. What's a me...mena-a...

MICHAEL
A ménage à trois, baby. Two's company—three's a ménage.

COWBOY
Oh.

HANK
It works for some.

LARRY
Well, I'm not one for group therapy. I'm sorry, I can't relate to anyone or anything that way. I'm old-fashioned—I like 'em all, but I like 'em one at a time!

MICHAEL
        [*To* LARRY]
Did you like Donald as a single side attraction?
        [*Pause*]

LARRY
Yes. I did.

DONALD
So did I, Larry.

LARRY
        [*To* DONALD, *referring to* MICHAEL]
Did you tell him?

114

DONALD
No.

MICHAEL
It was perfectly obvious from the moment you walked in. What was
the song and dance about having seen each other but never having
met?

DONALD
It was true. We saw each other in the baths and went to bed together,
but we never spoke a word and never knew each other's name.

EMORY
You have better luck than I do. If I don't get arrested, my trick
announces upon departure that he's been exposed to hepatitis!
One more shot of gamma globulin and my ass'll look like a pair of
colanders!

MICHAEL
In spring a young man's fancy turns to a fancy young man.

LARRY
    [*To HANK*]
Don't look at me like that. You've been playing footsie with the
Blue Book all night.

DONALD
I think he only wanted to show you what's good for the gander is
good for the gander.

HANK
That's right.

LARRY
    [*To HANK*]
I suppose you'd like the three of us to have a go at it.

HANK
At least it'd be together.

LARRY
That point eludes me.

HANK
What kind of an understanding do you *want!*

LARRY
Respect—for each other's freedom. With no need to lie or pretend. In my own way, Hank, I love you, but you have to understand that even though I do want to go on living with you, sometimes there may be others. I don't want to flaunt it in your face. If it happens, I know I'll never mention it. But if you ask me, I'll tell you. I don't want to hurt you, but I won't lie to you if you want to know anything about me.

BERNARD
He gets points.

MICHAEL
What?

BERNARD
He said it. He said "I love you" to Hank. He gets the bonus.

MICHAEL
He didn't call him.

DONALD
He called him. He just didn't use the telephone.

MICHAEL
Then he doesn't get any points.

BERNARD
He gets five points!

MICHAEL
He didn't use the telephone. He doesn't get a goddamn thing!
    [LARRY goes to the phone, picks up the receiver, looks at the number of the second line, dials. A beat. The phone rings]

LARRY
It's for you, Hank. Why don't you take it upstairs?
    [The phone continues to ring. HANK gets up, goes up the stairs to the bedroom. Pause. He presses the second-line button, picks up the receiver. Everyone downstairs is silent]

HANK
Hello?

BERNARD
One point.

116

LARRY
Hello, Hank.

BERNARD
Two points.

LARRY
...This is Larry.

BERNARD
Two more points!

LARRY
...For what it's worth, I love you.

BERNARD
Five points bonus!

HANK
I'll...I'll try.

LARRY
I will too.
        [*Hangs up.* HANK *hangs up*]

BERNARD
That's ten points total!

EMORY
Larry's the winner!

HAROLD
Well, that wasn't as much fun as I thought it would be.

MICHAEL
THE GAME ISN'T OVER YET!
        [HANK *moves toward the bed into darkness*]
Your turn, Alan.
        [MICHAEL *gets the phone, slams it down in front of* ALAN]
PICK UP THE PHONE, BUSTER!

EMORY
Michael, don't!

MICHAEL
STAY OUT OF THIS!

EMORY
You don't have to, Alan. You don't have to.

ALAN
Emory...I'm sorry for what I did before.
    [*A beat*]

EMORY
...Oh, forget it.

MICHAEL
Forgive us our trespasses. Christ, now you're both joined at the goddamn hip! You can decorate his home, Emory—and he can get you out of jail the next time you're arrested on a morals charge.
    [*A beat*]
Who are you going to call, Alan?
    [*No response*]
Can't remember anyone? Well, maybe you need a minute to think. Is that it?
    [*No response*]

HAROLD
I believe this will be the final round.

COWBOY
Michael, aren't you going to call anyone?

HAROLD
How could he? He's never loved anyone.

MICHAEL
    [*Sings the classic vaudeville walk-off to* HAROLD]
"No matter how you figger,
It's tough to be a nigger,
    [*Indicates* BERNARD]
But it's tougher
To be a Jeeeew-ooouu-oo!"

DONALD
My God, Michael, you're a charming host.

HAROLD
Michael doesn't have charm, Donald. Michael has counter-charm.
    [LARRY *crosses to the stairs*]

118

MICHAEL
Going somewhere?
> [*LARRY stops, turns to* MICHAEL]

LARRY
Yes. Excuse me.
> [*Turns, goes up the stairs*]

MICHAEL
You're going to miss the end of the game.

LARRY
> [*Pauses on stairs*]
You can tell me how it comes out.

MICHAEL
I never reveal an ending. And no one will be reseated during the climactic revelation.

LARRY
With any luck, I won't be back until it's all over.
> [*Turns, continues up the stairs into the dark*]

MICHAEL
> [*Into* ALAN'S *ear*]
What do you suppose is going on up there? Hmmm, Alan? What do you imagine Larry and Hank are doing? Hmmmmm? Shooting marbles?

EMORY
Whatever they're doing, they're not hurting anyone.

HAROLD
And they're minding their own business.

MICHAEL
And you mind yours, Harold. I'm warning you!
> [*A beat*]

HAROLD
> [*Coolly*]
Are you now? Are you warning *me? Me?* I'm Harold. I'm the one person you don't warn, Michael. Because you and I are a match. And we tread very softly with each other because we both play each other's game too well. Oh, I know this game you're playing.

George and Martha

HAROLD [*Cont'd*]
I know it very well. And I play it very well. You play it very well
too. But you know what, I'm the only one that's better at it than
you are. I can beat you at it. So don't push me. I'm warning *you*.
[*A beat.* MICHAEL *starts to laugh*]

MICHAEL
You're funny, Hallie. A laff riot. Isn't he funny, Alan? Or, as you
might say, isn't he amusing? He's an amusing faggot, isn't he? Or, as
you might say, freak. That's what you called Emory, wasn't it? A
freak? A pansy? My, what an antiquated vocabulary you have. I'm
surprised you didn't say sodomite or pederast.
[*A beat*]
You'd better let me bring you up to date. Now it's not so new, but it
might be new to you—
[*A beat*]
Have you heard the term "closet queen"? Do you know what that
means? Do you know what it means to be "in the closet"?

EMORY
Don't, Michael. It won't help anything to explain what it means.

MICHAEL
He already knows. He knows very, very well what a closet queen is.
Don't you, Alan?
[*Pause*]

ALAN
Michael, if you are insinuating that I am homosexual, I can only say
that you are mistaken.

MICHAEL
Am I?
[*A beat*]
What about Justin Stuart?

ALAN
…What about…Justin Stuart?

MICHAEL
You were in love with him, that's what about him.
[*A beat*]
And *that* is who you are going to call.

120

ALAN

Justin and I were very good friends. That is all. Unfortunately, we had a parting of the ways and that was the end of the friendship. We have not spoken for years. I most certainly will not call him now.

MICHAEL

According to Justin, the friendship was quite passionate.

ALAN

What do you mean?

MICHAEL

I mean that you slept with him in college. Several times.

ALAN

That is not true!

MICHAEL

Several times. One time, it's youth. Twice, a phase maybe. Several times, *you like it!*

ALAN

IT'S NOT TRUE!

MICHAEL

Yes, it is. Because Justin Stuart *is* homosexual. He comes to New York on occasion. He calls me. I've taken him to parties. Larry "had" him once. *I* have slept with Justin Stuart. And he has told me all about *you.*

ALAN

Then he told you a lie.
    [*A beat*]

MICHAEL

You were obsessed with Justin. That's all you talked about, morning, noon, and night. You started doing it about Hank upstairs tonight. What an attractive fellow he is and all that transparent crap.

ALAN

He *is* an attractive fellow. What's wrong with saying so?

MICHAEL

Would you like to join him and Larry right now?

ALAN
I said he was attractive. That's all.

MICHAEL
How many times do you have to say it? How many times did you
have to say it about Justin: what a good tennis player he was; what
a good dancer he was; what a good body he had; what good taste
he had; how bright he was—how *amusing* he was—how the girls
were all mad for him—what close friends you were.

ALAN
We...we...were...very close...very good...friends. *That's all.*

MICHAEL
It was *obvious*—and when you did it around Fran it was downright
embarrassing. Even she must have had her doubts about you.

ALAN
Justin...lied. If he told you that, he lied. It is a lie. A vicious lie.
He'd say anything about me now to get even. He could never get
over the fact that *I* dropped *him*. But I had to. I had to because...he
told me...he told me about himself...he told me that he wanted to
be my lover. And I...I...told him...he made me sick...I told him I
pitied him.
    [*A beat*]

MICHAEL
You ended the friendship, Alan, because you couldn't face the truth
about yourself. You could go along, sleeping with Justin, as long as
he lied to himself and you lied to yourself and you both dated girls
and labeled yourselves men and called yourselves just fond friends.
But Justin finally had to be honest about the truth, and you couldn't
take it. You couldn't take it and so you destroyed the friendship and
your friend along with it.
    [*MICHAEL goes to the desk and gets address book*]

ALAN
No!

MICHAEL
Justin could never understand what he'd done wrong to make you
cut him off. He blamed himself.

ALAN
No!

122

MICHAEL
He did until he eventually found out who he was and what he was.

ALAN
No!

MICHAEL
But to this day he still remembers the treatment—the scars he got from you.
        [*Puts address book in front of* ALAN *on coffee table*]

ALAN
NO!

MICHAEL
Pick up this phone and call Justin. Call him and apologize and tell him what you should have told him twelve years ago.
        [*Picks up the phone, shoves it at* ALAN]

ALAN
NO! HE LIED! NOT A WORD IS TRUE!

MICHAEL
CALL HIM!
        [ALAN *won't take the phone*]
All right then, *I'll dial!*

HAROLD
You're so helpful.
        [MICHAEL *starts to dial*]

ALAN
Give it to me.
        [MICHAEL *hands* ALAN *the receiver.* ALAN *takes it, hangs up for a moment, lifts it again, starts to dial. Everyone watches silently.* ALAN *finishes dialing, lifts the receiver to his ear*]
...Hello?

MICHAEL
One point.

ALAN
...It's...it's Alan.

MICHAEL
Two points.

ALAN
…Yes, yes, it's *me*.

MICHAEL
Is it Justin?

ALAN
…You sound surprised.

MICHAEL
I should hope to think so—after twelve years! Two more points.

ALAN
I…I'm in New York. Yes. I…I won't explain now… I…I just called to tell you…

MICHAEL
THAT I LOVE YOU, GODDAMNIT! I LOVE YOU!

ALAN
I love you.

MICHAEL
You get the goddamn bonus. TEN POINTS TOTAL! JACKPOT!

ALAN
I love you and I beg you to forgive me.

MICHAEL
Give me that!
        [*Snatches the phone from* ALAN]
Justin! Did you hear what that son of a bitch said!
        [*A beat.* MICHAEL *is speechless for a moment*]
…Fran?
        [*A beat*]
Well, of course I expected it to be you!…
        [*A beat*]
How are you? Me too. Yes, yes…he told me everything. Oh, don't thank *me*. Please… Please…
        [*A beat*]
I'll…I'll put him back on.
        [*A beat*]
My love to the kids…

124

ALAN

...Darling? I'll take the first plane I can get. Yes. I'm sorry too. I love you very much.

[*Hangs up, stands, crosses to the door, stops. Turns around, surveys the group*]

Thank you, Michael.

[*Opens the door and exits. Silence.* MICHAEL *slowly sinks down on the couch, covering his face. Pause*]

COWBOY

Who won?

DONALD

It was a tie.

[HAROLD *crosses to* MICHAEL]

HAROLD

[*Calmly, coldly, clinically*]

Now it is my turn. And ready or not, Michael, here goes.

[*A beat*]

You are a sad and pathetic man. You're a homosexual and you don't want to be. But there is nothing you can do to change it. Not all your prayers to your God, not all the analysis you can buy in all the years you've got left to live. You may very well one day be able to know a heterosexual life if you want it desperately enough—if you pursue it with the fervor with which you annihilate—but you will always be homosexual as well. Always, Michael. Always. Until the day you die.

[*Turns, gathers his gifts, goes to* EMORY. EMORY *stands up unsteadily*]

Oh, friends, thanks for the nifty party and the super gift.

[*Looks toward* COWBOY]

It's just what I needed.

[EMORY *smiles.* HAROLD *gives him a hug, spots* BERNARD *sitting on the floor, head bowed*]

...Bernard, thank you.

[*No response. To* EMORY]

Will you get him home?

EMORY

Don't worry about her. I'll take care of everything.

[HAROLD *turns to* DONALD, *who is at the bar making himself another drink*]

HAROLD
Donald, good to see you.

DONALD
Good night, Harold. See you again sometime.

HAROLD
Yeah. How about a year from Shavuoth?
    [*HAROLD goes to* COWBOY]
Come on, Tex. Let's go to my place.
    [COWBOY *gets up, comes to him*]
Are you good in bed?

COWBOY
Well...I'm not like the average hustler you'd meet. I try to show a
little affection—it keeps me from feeling like such a whore.
    [*A beat.* HAROLD *turns.* COWBOY *opens the door for them. They start
    out.* HAROLD *pauses*]

HAROLD
Oh, Michael...thanks for the laughs. Call you tomorrow.
    [*No response. A beat.* HAROLD *and* COWBOY *exit*]

EMORY
Come on, Bernard. Time to go home.
    [EMORY, *frail as he is, manages to pull* BERNARD's *arm around his
    neck, gets him on his feet*]
Oh, Mary, you're a heavy mother.

BERNARD
    [*Practically inaudible mumble*]
Why did I call? Why?

EMORY
Thank you, Michael. Good night, Donald.

DONALD
Goodbye, Emory.

BERNARD
Why...

EMORY
It's all right, Bernard. Everything's all right. I'm going to make you
some coffee and everything's going to be all right.

[EMORY *virtually carries* BERNARD *out.* DONALD *closes the door. Silence.* MICHAEL *slowly slips from the couch onto the floor. A beat. Then slowly he begins a low moan that increases in volume—almost like a siren. Suddenly he slams his open hands to his ears*]

MICHAEL
[*In desperate panic*]
Donald! Donald! DONALD! DONALD!
[DONALD *puts down his drink, rushes to* MICHAEL. MICHAEL *is now white with fear, and tears are bursting from his eyes. He begins to gasp his words*]
Oh, no! No! What have I done! Oh, my God, what have I done!
[MICHAEL *writhing.* DONALD *holds him, cradles him in his arms*]

DONALD
Michael! Michael!

MICHAEL
[*Weeping*]
Oh, no! NO! It's beginning! The liquor is starting to wear off and the anxiety is beginning! Oh, NO! No! I feel it! I know it's going to happen. Donald!! Donald! Don't leave me! Please! Please! Oh, my God, what have I done! Oh, Jesus, the guilt! I can't handle it anymore. I won't make it!

DONALD
[*Physically subduing him*]
Michael! Michael! Stop it! Stop it! I'll give you a Valium—I've got some in my pocket!

MICHAEL
[*Hysterical*]
No! No! Pills and alcohol—I'll die!

DONALD
I'm not going to give you the whole bottle! Come on, let go of me!

MICHAEL
[*Clutching him*]
NO!

DONALD
Let go of me long enough for me to get my hand in my pocket!

127

MICHAEL
Don't leave!
> [*MICHAEL quiets down a bit, lets go of* DONALD *enough for him to take a small plastic bottle from his pocket and open it to give* MICHAEL *a tranquilizer*]

DONALD
Here.

MICHAEL
> [*Sobbing*]

I don't have any water to swallow it with!

DONALD
Well, if you'll wait one goddamn minute, I'll get you some!
> [*MICHAEL lets go of him. He goes to the bar, gets a glass of water and returns*]

Your water, your Majesty.
> [*A beat*]

Michael, stop that goddamn crying and take this pill!
> [*MICHAEL straightens up, puts the pill into his mouth amid choking sobs, takes the water, drinks, returns the glass to* DONALD]

MICHAEL
I'm like Ole Man River—tired of livin' and scared o' dyin'.
> [DONALD *puts the glass on the bar, comes back to the couch, sits down.* MICHAEL *collapses into his arms, sobbing. Pause*]

DONALD
Shhhhh. Shhhhhh. Michael. Shhhhhh. Michael. Michael.
> [DONALD *rocks him back and forth. He quiets. Pause*]

MICHAEL
...If we...if we could just...not hate ourselves so much. That's it, you know. If we could just *learn* not to hate ourselves quite so very much.

DONALD
Yes, I know. I know.
> [*A beat*]

Inconceivable as it may be, you used to be worse than you are now.
> [*A beat*]

Maybe with a lot more work you can help yourself some more—if you try.
> [*MICHAEL straightens up, dries his eyes on his sleeve*]

MICHAEL

Who was it that used to always say, "You show me a happy homosexual, and I'll show you a gay corpse"?

DONALD

I don't know. Who was it who always used to say that?

MICHAEL

And how dare you come on with that holier-than-thou attitude with me! "A lot more work," "if I try," indeed! You've got a long row to hoe before you're perfect, you know.

DONALD

I never said I didn't.

MICHAEL

And while we're on the subject—I think your analyst is a quack.
    [MICHAEL *is sniffling.* DONALD *hands him a handkerchief. He takes it and blows his nose*]

DONALD

Earlier you said he was a prick.

MICHAEL

That's right. He's a prick quack. Or a quack prick, whichever you prefer.
    [DONALD *gets up from the couch, goes for his drink*]

DONALD

    [*Heaving a sigh*]
Harold was right. You'll never change.

MICHAEL

Come back, Donald. Come back, Shane.

DONALD

I'll come back when you have another anxiety attack.

MICHAEL

I need you. Just like Mickey Mouse needs Minnie Mouse—just like Donald Duck needs Minnie Duck. Mickey needs Donnie.

DONALD

My name is Donald. I am called Donald. You must never call anyone called Donald Donnie...

MICHAEL
[*Grabs his head, moans*]
Ohhhhh…icks! Icks! Terrible icks! Tomorrow is going to be an ick-packed day. It's going to be a bad day at Black Rock. A day of nerves, nerves, and more nerves!
[*MICHAEL gets up from the couch, surveys the wreckage of the dishes and gift wrappings*]
Do you suppose there's any possibility of just burning this room?
[*A beat*]

DONALD
Why do you think he stayed, Michael? Why do you think he took all of that from you?

MICHAEL
There are no accidents. He was begging to get killed. He was dying for somebody to let him have it and he got what he wanted.

DONALD
He could have been telling the truth—Justin could have lied.

MICHAEL
Who knows? What time is it?

DONALD
It seems like it's day after tomorrow.
[*MICHAEL goes to the kitchen door, pokes his head in. Comes back into the room carrying a raincoat*]

MICHAEL
It's early.
[*Goes to a closet door, takes out a blazer, puts it on*]

DONALD
What does life *hold?* Where're you going?

MICHAEL
The bedroom is ocupado, and I don't want to go to sleep anyway until I try to walk off the booze. If I went to sleep like this, when I wake up they'd have to put me in a padded cell—not that that's where I don't belong.
[*A beat*]
And…and…there's a midnight mass at St. Malachy's that all the show people go to. I think I'll walk over there and catch it.

130

DONALD
[*Raises his glass*]
Well, pray for me.

MICHAEL
[*Indicates bedroom*]
Maybe they'll be gone by the time I get back.

DONALD
Well, *I* will be—just as soon as I knock off that bottle of brandy.

MICHAEL
Will I see you next Saturday?

DONALD
Unless you have other plans.

MICHAEL
No.
[*Turns to go*]

DONALD
Michael?

MICHAEL
[*Stops, turns back*]
What?

DONALD
Did he ever tell you why he was crying on the phone—what it was he *had* to tell you?

MICHAEL
No. It must have been that he'd left Fran. Or maybe it was something else and he changed his mind.

DONALD
Maybe so.
[*A beat*]
I wonder why he left her.
[*A pause*]

MICHAEL
...As my father said to me when he died in my arms, "I don't understand any of it. I never did."

[*A beat.* DONALD *goes to his stack of books, selects one, and sits in a chair*]
Turn out the lights when you leave, will you?

[DONALD *nods.* MICHAEL *looks at him for a long silent moment.* DONALD *turns his attention to his book, starts to read.* MICHAEL *opens the door and exits*]

END OF ACT 2

END OF PLAY

THE MEN FROM THE BOYS

A SEQUEL PLAY

FOR

TRICIA GUILD

AND

RICHARD POLO

§   §   §

The Men From the Boys had its world premiere at The
New Conservatory Theatre Center, San Francisco,
(Ed Decker, Artistic Director) on October 26, 2002.
The scene design was by Eric Sinkkonen, the music
by Larry Grossman, and the stage manager was
Phillip Lienau. The play was produced and directed
by Ed Decker. The cast was:

DONALD	Peter Carlstrom
MICHAEL	Russ Duffy
EMORY	Michael Patrick Gaffney
SCOTT	Olen Christian Holm
HAROLD	Will Huddleston
HANK	Terry Lamb
RICK	Rajiv Shah
BERNARD	Lewis Sims
JASON	Owen Thomas

S p e c i a l   t h a n k s   t o :

Andrew Nance
(Actor, Conservatory Director)
and
Buddy Thomas
(playwright, agent
who brought TMFTB to TNCTC)

Keri Fitch (costumes), Melissa Kalstrom (wigs, hair, and makeup),
Victoria Kirby (publicity), Nancy Mancias (properties), Jonathan
Retsky (lighting), and Steve Romanko (sound design).

TNCTC and the author wish to acknowledge
Mr. Steven Buss
and also
Mr. Arnold Stiefel
of Stiefel Entertainment
for their individual support and generosity.

A c t   1

THE SET: A deliberate reproduction of the concept for an East 50s Manhattan duplex (bedroom upstairs), designed by Peter Harvey for THE BOYS IN THE BAND: a black-and-white photo blowup collage of chic rooms (as seen in interior decor magazines), which completely covers all wall surfaces. Abstract and stylish.

In the original production there were only "Deco" black Naugahyde chrome tube chairs, a settee, and a couple of chrome and glass side tables. That was it. In any case, the effect should be deliberately minimal, monochromatic, and clean-lined, without a single unnecessary item of dressing. Dramatic and anal. And, of course, it should positively scream "taste."

From a state of complete darkness the lights suddenly illuminate full-tilt to reveal a stage occupied by five characters from *The Boys in the Band,* now thirty years older but still pulled together. Their ages (and the state of their hair) are: MICHAEL, fifty-nine, thin-ish or a meticulous, studied comb-over; EMORY, sixty-two, dyed auburn; BERNARD, fifty-seven, salt and pepper; DONALD, fifty-seven, blond/silver; and HANK, sixty-one, distinguished gray temples. HAROLD, sixty-one, with receding curly black hair, will enter eventually.

This quintet is positioned formally at various interesting levels: standing with hands in pockets or arms folded; seated on a chair or a stool or the stairs. They all look directly at the audience, completely poker-faced (Sad? Dazed? Imperious?), as if caught in an artfully composed still of the early Avedon/Stern school. All wear suits or jackets and ties: Emory in a Charvet bow cravat and black velour suit (minus the jacket); Michael in a charcoal-gray flannel two-piece Armani and solid charcoal tie. Donald, alone, has loosened his striped rep, unfastened his button-down collar, and removed his navy Brooks Brothers blazer to sling it over his shoulder.

The "men" of the title are lit in hotter pools of light than the three new "boys," who face upstage with their backs to the audience. They are SCOTT, twenty-six, JASON, thirty-something, both Caucasian; and RICK, twenty-four, an Asian-American.

They are all dressed in more relaxed, up-to-the-minute styles, from slacks and pullovers to jeans and jackets with T-shirts. They are scattered among the originals, posed in more casual attitudes: draped against the stairs, lolling on the back of the sofa, or lying on the floor, propped on an arm. Their facial attitudes are concealed, but their body language varies from studied casual to subtly provocative.

After the "shock illumination" of the frieze, there is what seems to be an interminable pause. We hear only the SOUND of heavy rain and EMORY'S delicately pulling a needle and yarn through a small, unfinished, petit point pattern. The dimmer circles of light sneak to the level of the hotter ones. No one moves or speaks. The older characters continue to stare straight forward, enigmatic; the younger ones remain turned away, their attitudes unknown. Then, just as the audience is about to break with restless nervousness, in reaction to the prolonged silence, stillness, and scrutiny, EMORY starts to cough uncontrollably. Everyone else slowly, deliberately turns his head without moving his body to glare at EMORY (Disapprovingly? Sympathetically? Affectlessly?) and hold until EMORY calms, heavily clears his throat.

Finally, EMORY sheepishly scans the sea of attention, chagrined at everyone looking at him…

    EMORY
        [*Tongue-in-cheek*]
It must be the excitement. We're having too much fun here.

        [*No one cracks a smile. Not a titter. They all continue to look at*
        EMORY *a moment longer (Contempt? Compassion? Indifference?),*
        then DONALD *breaks the mood, flings his blazer aside, goes to a bar*
        cart, and pours a crystal tumbler of water from a pitcher.]

    MICHAEL
        [*Sardonically*]
Excitement, indeed! Some "celebration of life"! It's so fucking quiet in here, you could hear boll weevils pissing on cotton!

    DONALD
        [*Palm to ear*]
Listen! I think I hear them! No, it's just pissing with rain.

    MICHAEL
Let's have some music, Bernard. Liven up this taffy-pull.

BERNARD
[*Facetiously*]
Sure. I'll just put on a little gangsta rap.
[*BERNARD goes to an étagère, begins to shuffle through some CDs.*]

MICHAEL
[*Dryly, offhand*]
You do and there's gonna be some strange fruit hangin' from the poplar trees.
[*EMORY, with an arched "Ahem!" clears his throat at MICHAEL'S "wit." RICK, the exotically attractive Asian-American, speaks up.*]

RICK
[*To MICHAEL*]
Is that a racist remark?

BERNARD
[*Weary, tongue-in-cheek*]
Well, Michael's not exactly out in a cornfield at midnight, burning crosses. His ambivalent generation of so-called Southern liberals has just got to die out.
[*Dryly*]
It shouldn't be long now.
[*Meanwhile, DONALD has crossed to EMORY, hands him a tumbler.*]

DONALD
Here, Emory, drink some water.

EMORY
Is it bottled or just from the tap?

MICHAEL
[*Quickly, an edge*]
It's from the toilet. It's toilet water. Every morning I submerge an empty Evian bottle in the toilet. It's multipurpose eau de toilette—you can either drink it or put it behind your ears.
[*EMORY shoots MICHAEL a withering look, takes a sip from the tumbler, returns it to DONALD.*]

EMORY
[*Sweetly*]
Thanks, Donald. You're a real sis'.
[*This remark is met with some audible groans from JASON, BERNARD, and DONALD. (Note: There is an open bottle of Dom Perignon in a wine cooler on the cart and HANK and RICK take a sip champagne from flutes already in their hands.)*]

[*Everyone begins to shift, get up, and move about. All except* SCOTT, *the loner with the knockout good looks, who noticeably remains apart from the group—perhaps leaning on the far side of the stairs, hands in pockets, staring into space.*]

BERNARD
  [*Generally, re* EMORY]
Wouldn't you know she only drinks designer water.

EMORY
Don't say "she"! You, of all people, know that's *not* politically correct!
  [*Big flirty smile to* JASON]
Is it, Jason?

BERNARD
  [*Quickly, to* EMORY]
Calling people "sis" is not exactly *enlightened.*
  [JASON, *proletariat activist, gym-body, sexy in an obvious way, turns at the mention of his name…*]

JASON
It's all right, Emory. We make allowances for those who have gone before.

EMORY
  [*Drawing himself up*]
Do I detect the remotest innuendo that I am slightly older than you?

JASON
  [*To* EMORY]
You planted the redwoods, didn't you?
  [*Some scattered laughter.* EMORY *makes a quick decision to take the high road…*]

EMORY
  [*To* JASON, *mock-insulted*]
Oh, you're *terrible!*
  [*Coy, a beat*]
But I like you.
  [JASON *looks indifferent, turns away.* EMORY *recovers with a certain practiced (and practical) dignity, joins* BERNARD *at the étagère to select CDs.*]

DONALD
Did you know the UN declared this "The Year of the Older Person"?

JASON
I'm glad they declared *something*.

MICHAEL
[*Still on earlier thought*]
I *am* the most liberal Confederate who ever lived! Why, when I was sixteen my father gave me a convertible, and do you know my best friend was a black gay boy. Oh, he'd have to sit in the back seat, of course, so no one would say anything. It was the acceptable, hypocritical, *idiotic* way things were done.

BERNARD
If you'd had any guts, you'd have made him sit up front.

MICHAEL
Then he'd have looked like the chauffeur.

BERNARD
In the *passenger* seat *beside* you!

MICHAEL
Funny thing, Bernard, dear. Neither of us wanted our balls between a split rail. We were smart. *We played the system.*

JASON
Somebody has to put their balls on the line sometime.

MICHAEL
[*Re empty flutes*]
Jason, why don't you *act up* like the old days and freshen everyone's drinks? You're so good at it.

JASON
That's why I'm a bartender *these* days!

MICHAEL
Oh, well, if you're offended and going to picket or protest this solemn occasion, then...
[*JASON ignores MICHAEL, goes to the bar cart as RICK...*]

RICK
[*To EMORY*]
You're the first real interior decorator I've ever been around.

EMORY
Designer. We prefer interior *"designer."* Like flight attendants prefer "flight attendant" instead of "stewardess."

JASON
Or "steward," if you happen to be a man.

EMORY
[*Quick and pointed*]
So few are.

BERNARD
[*To JASON*]
You've had more careers than anybody I know.

JASON
[*Refills his flute*]
Mmm, I've careered from career to career, to quote somebody, and guess what?

MICHAEL
You're still queer.

JASON
I'm still a major fuck-up.

DONALD
[*Crosses to JASON*]
I thought I held that title.

BERNARD
Why *not* go into politics? Being a fuck-up seems to be a prerequisite.

JASON
I'm too old for that. Haven't got a law degree and haven't got the money to get one. Had to drop out, as it was.
[*To DONALD*]
What can I do for you, sir?

DONALD
[*Bit too flirtatious*]
Beer. No, a glass of white wine. No an extra dry Bombay martini on the rocks, please?

EMORY
Beer! Wine! Booze! Make up your mind! It's readiness that
makes a woman!
> [*He is ignored by everyone.*]

JASON
More champagne, Hank?

HANK
No, thanks.

JASON
> [*Re empty bucket*]
We need ice.

MICHAEL
There's no ice? I thought...

DONALD
> [*Picks up bucket*]
I'll get it.

SCOTT
I'll get it. Sorry.
> [*DONALD stops. Everyone reacts to SCOTT having spoken. He goes to
> DONALD, takes the silver ice bucket.*]

DONALD
> [*To SCOTT*]
You don't mind doing it?

SCOTT
> [*For MICHAEL's benefit*]
I'll do anything if I'm not humiliated.

MICHAEL
> [*To SCOTT, calmly, seriously*]
Did I humiliate you? Have I *ever* humiliated you?
> [*No answer*]
Well?
> [*SCOTT exits off left to kitchen.*]
I guess that was a rhetorical question.

EMORY
[*CDs in hand*]
So, what are we going to do, kids? Put on some music and dance our tits off?

DONALD
[*Moving away*]
I'd rather be in a ditch.

EMORY
[*Ever the fun one*]
Well, then, I just heard about this marvelous new party game! Everyone takes his clothes off and forms two parallel lines, facing each other. And then, when someone yells "Go!" the two lines make a mad stampede toward each other...and the first one that gets in gets a kiss!
[*He breaks himself up, laughing. Nobody else cracks a smile, they all just glare at him again.*]

EMORY
[*Trying to save the moment*]
I forgot to say condoms are passed out first. Does that make it funnier?
[*Silence*]
Okay, why don't we all just pull on our wet suits and grovel around on top of each other?

MICHAEL
[*Grimly, calmly*]
There will be no dancing. There will be no games played. And for the duration of this event, no one is allowed to take off so much as a necktie. For that, you'll have to see some *serious* gay theater. All-male nude Chekhov, that sort of thing.

BERNARD
[*To EMORY*]
No nudity tonight. Not with *this* crowd.
[*Looks at JASON*]
Well, not with *most* of this crowd.

RICK
[*Re earlier thought*]
I'm glad we're not gonna play that game!

EMORY
[*To* RICK, *sympathetically*]
Me, too, actually. Because of a few unwanted kilos. But, I'll soon
have a new bod. I now have a personal trainer, and he's marvelous.
He said to me, "First we lose the weight, then we sculpt."

BERNARD
That ought to be as simple as chopping a fifth face on Mount
Rushmore.

EMORY
I've lost four pounds! Can't you tell?

DONALD
Not from this angle.

BERNARD
[*Re music*]
Whatta you want, Michael?
[*Quickly*]
EllaMabelJudyPeggyBarbra—or Bobby?

MICHAEL
You know I don't own any Streisand.

EMORY
[*Holding up a CD*]
Yes, you do, right here, the one that's got "When in Rome" on it.

MICHAEL
That belongs to Harold.

JASON
Is there anything that was written in the last forty years?
[*MICHAEL gives* JASON *a look as* SCOTT *enters with the filled bucket.*
BERNARD *puts on something like Chet Baker's recording of "Tenderly."*]

JASON
[*To* SCOTT, *taking bucket*]
Thanks, Scott. What'll it be?

SCOTT
[*Dryly*]
I'll have some of that toilet water. With a twist.
[*JASON puts some ice in the martini he has made, hands it to* DONALD.]

JASON
Donald.

DONALD
Thanks.
>[*JASON pours SCOTT an Evian. SCOTT returns to the outer limits by the stairs.*]

DONALD
>[*Sips drink, reacts*]
Oh, yeah, Jason, that's good.

JASON
>[*Smiles noncommitally*]
Thank you, sir.
>[*JASON walks away from the bar cart with a can of Diet Coke just as EMORY says…*]

EMORY
I'd like some coffee.
>[*JASON pops the top of the Diet Coke can and drinks. EMORY forces a stiff smile at being ignored. RICK puts down his drink, picks up a silver coffeepot and cup and saucer from the bar cart.*]

RICK
>[*Pleasantly, to EMORY re coffee*]
How do you like it?

EMORY
>[*Campily sultry*]
Like I like my men.

BERNARD
>[*To EMORY, re RICK*]
Sorry, he ain't got no gay coffee!

EMORY
>[*Snaps*]
I meant hot and café au lait!

BERNARD
He knows what you meant. And he still doesn't give a shit.
>[*EMORY sucks a tooth, nose in the air. RICK picks up the silver coffeepot, looks at it appreciatively.*]

RICK
[*Ingenuously, not a trace of chichi*]
What a nice coffeepot. Nice and simple, you know.
[*RICK pours EMORY a cup...*]

EMORY
And a lovely ice bucket too. Really too lovely for ice.
[*To MICHAEL*]
You ought to float a pansy in it.

MICHAEL
[*"Menacingly"*]
I might just do that. Facedown.
[*RICK hands the coffee to EMORY...*]

RICK
[*Pleasantly*]
There you go, Emory.

EMORY
[*Taking the cup, with flirty charm*]
Merci, mille fois.

RICK
[*Innocently*]
Oh, you speak French?

EMORY
No, I was just... Well, it's hard to explain exactly. It's what used to
be called *charm*. Of course, that was a while back.
[*A look to JASON*]
Only those who've "gone before" might remember.

RICK
[*Back a beat, to EMORY*]
I just thought with a name like Em-or-ee...and café au lait...
[*re MICHAEL*]
...and him saying the thing about Evian...and...
[*French pronunciation of Evian: Aye-vee-anh*]

MICHAEL
[*Tolerantly*]
I have a name too, and it's not *him*, it's Michael.

RICK
[*Conciliatory*]
Sorry.
[*Continuing, to* EMORY]
And MICHAEL here, saying the thing about...well, I don't know, I
just thought you might be French or something. 'Cause *I* speak
French.
[EMORY *is silent, thinking this over.*]

MICHAEL
[*To* EMORY]
Did you follow that? Or were you knocked senseless by *The Great
Language Barrier Reef of Time*?

EMORY
[*To* RICK, *simply*]
Emory was my mother's family name, and she wasn't French. At
least if she was she never told *me*.

RICK
My mother *was* French. Well, French-Vietnamese.

MICHAEL
[*To* RICK, *slightly grand*]
I don't believe we've been formally introduced.

RICK
[*Extends his hand*]
Oh, I should have introduced myself.

MICHAEL
I mean, you *look* familiar, but...

RICK
[*Shakes hands with* MICHAEL]
I'm out of uniform.
[MICHAEL *reacts oddly, takes this in.*]

HANK
[*To* RICK]
Well, *I* know you. I remember you nights—mostly nights.

RICK
[*To* MICHAEL]
Yeah, the graveyard shift. I'm a practical nurse. Part-time.

MICHAEL
Oh, of course you are!

RICK
[*Tentatively*]
When Larry couldn't sleep, we'd talk—or I'd just hold his hand.
We...became quite close. He gave me some of his artwork...stuff he
had in his room. And some books.
[*To* HANK]
I hope you don't mind.

HANK
Why should I? They were his things.

RICK
[*To* MICHAEL]
I know I wasn't exactly invited, but I thought it was kind of an
open house...

MICHAEL
[*Chagrined*]
Oh, it *is*. Why, you're *very, very* welcome, Rick. I just don't remember you. I wasn't there much in the evening, but then, Larry tended
to keep people in his life rather compartmentalized.

JASON
It's kind of a gay thing, don't you think?

SCOTT
[*Involuntarily*]
Yeah. Friends, anyway.

MICHAEL
[*"Graciously"*]
Well, now, Rick...what do you do when you're not *nursing*?

RICK
I'm an art student. Part-time. Larry encouraged me to enroll in
Parsons. He said if I'd go he'd pay for my tuition.

MICHAEL
I see.
[HANK *reacts with mild surprise.* BERNARD *looks to* HANK. MICHAEL
looks to SCOTT (*who turns away*), *then to* DONALD.]

149

MICHAEL
[*Remembers; generally*]
Oh, uh, there are some hot hors d'oeuvres! I don't know where my
mind is.

DONALD
[*Re SCOTT*]
I do.
[*MICHAEL shoots DONALD a look.*]

EMORY
[*To RICK; French pronunciation for "design"*]
Michael had Cuisine "Duhzine" do the food! I love their takeout!
They make the best vol-au-vent.
[*RICK stares at him blankly. (NOTE: the name of the caterer is
"Cuisine Design, but pronounced, as if, in French.)*]

BERNARD
Do real men eat vol-au-vent?

EMORY
[*Getting up, sighs*]
Well, if no one else is going to do it... So what else is nouvelle?

MICHAEL
Don't use the microwave.

EMORY
[*Very American accent*]
Jamais, cheri. It dries 'em out.
[*EMORY exits to the kitchen.*]

BERNARD
[*To MICHAEL*]
Is Larry's mother coming?

MICHAEL
[*Shakes his head*]
Had to get back to Philadelphia.

HANK
The older brother never liked me. He "disapproved." I called
him when Larry got so sick, but it was the same old story. I'm not
surprised he didn't show. But Larry's mother and stepfather managed to get here before he died. They stayed with us...I mean,
with me.

[*BERNARD comes over to* HANK, *puts his arm around him, and comforts him. The group watches stoically.*]

HANK
[*Quietly appreciative*]
Thanks, Bernard. This may sound strange, but you know, even after all these years I can't say I really knew Larry all that well. Do you find that some sort of demented statement?

BERNARD
No.

SCOTT
[*To no one in particular*]
Who ever knows anybody? You never know what's really going on with someone.

HANK
[*Absently*]
Yeah.
[MICHAEL *takes note of* SCOTT's *remark.*]

BERNARD
I think we always keep some part of ourselves *to* ourselves.

HANK
Larry had his secrets, of course. But that, in its way, had its allure. He was always a little bit of a mystery to me. And, I think, to a degree, to himself too.

BERNARD
I sure don't think I know myself.

JASON
Does anyone, really?

BERNARD
I mean...I don't think I can *explain* myself.

HANK
I know that even at my age I'm still finding out things about myself.

RICK

Me too. Now that it's over, I feel relief. And that's the truth. I feel so *relieved* that the nightmare is finally fucking over.

> [*A moment of silence.* EMORY *enters with a silver tray of canapés. All heads swivel to him (a repeat of the opening tableau when he coughed). The room is hushed. All heads follow* EMORY *as he crosses to* HANK.]

EMORY

> [*To* HANK]

Doughnut, soldier? Sorry, *finger* food?

HANK

> [*Has to laugh*]

No, thanks, Emory.

> [EMORY *passes among the group.*]

EMORY

Cheese puffs? Meatballs? Rumaki? If that dates me, how about: cellulars, nicotine patches, sex toys?

RICK

> [*Re tray of food*]

Very artistic, Emory. The presentation.

EMORY

I'm a born stylist.

> [*There are reactions of "Mmmm." Some take a canapé and a paper napkin from him, some do not. He comes to* MICHAEL, *who does not take anything, just stares icily at him…*]

MICHAEL

You used the microwave, didn't you?

EMORY

No, I didn't.

MICHAEL

Liar.

HANK

> [*Picking up thought*]

The time had long since past when we were physical with each other, but emotionally, we couldn't have been closer. He wanted to die. And he wanted me to *help* him die.

RICK
[*To* HANK]
And did you?

HANK
I would never be able to go on living with myself if I'd actually fed him the pills. That's funny, because I think I'm capable of *anything*—even killing someone. Anyway, I agreed to be with him— stay with him up to the point where he would swallow them—but I told him I wanted to leave before he did.

JASON
You have to be so careful of the fucking law.

HANK
I said I'd give him a scrambled egg so there'd be a little something in his stomach—give him a Dramamine so that he wouldn't vomit and strangle. But he'd have to actually *do* it himself. Swallow the pills alone. But in the end he didn't.

MICHAEL
[*Looks at his watch*]
Oh, where the hell is Harold?!

JASON
He must be caught in the rain.

EMORY
Oh, rain or shine, Harold'll be late for his *own* memorial.

BERNARD
I saw him at the service. Didn't you see him, Donald?

DONALD
[*Nods*]
With something very blond. Well, from the neck up.
[*The front door buzzer sounds...*]

MICHAEL
Speak of the devil.
[*MICHAEL goes to the panel beside the front door down right, presses a release button, tears opens the door, and goes out into the hallway.*]

HANK
[*To no one in particular*]
Larry conned every doctor in town out of pills. He made sure he
had a stash. He never told anybody, and he never took them. Not a
single one. But he made sure he had them...and yet, he wouldn't
take them. —Explain that.

EMORY
I'd have had Kevorkian on the speed dial.
    [*MICHAEL returns.*]

EMORY
Is it Hallie?

MICHAEL
No, it's the super. Scott, did you chain your bike in the entry?

SCOTT
Yeah, to the radiator. Why, is it in the way?

MICHAEL
He wants to mop up the rainwater or something. Bring it up here.
    [*SCOTT puts his glass on the stair rung, crosses, and goes out.*
    MICHAEL shuts the door.]

HANK
[*Weeps*]
Forgive me, I seem to be the only one wallowing in this.

DONALD
Don't be ridiculous, Hank.
    [*BERNARD helps sit HANK down, takes HANK's handkerchief out of
    his jacket pocket, and dries his eyes for him.*]

HANK
[*Re his tears*]
I'm sorry, I really am. This is supposed to be a celebration of life.

EMORY
Frankly, if I never attend another "celebration of life" as long as I
live, it'll be too fucking soon! And *if* I receive another invitation to a
"celebration of life," I *hope* there's a scratch-and-sniff cyanide cap-
sule enclosed! These postfuneral "cocktail huddles" only make you
wonder who's next!

BERNARD
How can you say such a thing!

EMORY
I'm just saying for *me*, all these things have begun to blur. I know it sounds polit...

MICHAEL
If you say "politically incorrect," I'm going to rip out your tongue and slice it for sandwiches.
     [*The sound of a key in the lock in the front door is heard. The door is opened by* SCOTT, *who rolls his bike inside and recloses it.*]

     [*He leans it against the wall.* JASON *crosses to the bike, stoops to "investigate" it.*]

JASON
     [*Re* SCOTT'*s bike*]
There's not a mark on it. Looks just like it did the night I sold it to you. From the way you were talking, I thought...

SCOTT
It's just the idea that it was stolen out of my apartment that made me feel so...

JASON
Maybe one of your friends was just a playing a trick on you. After all, it was returned to you.

SCOTT
I found it in the foyer of my building. Lying under the stairs, like it'd been dumped.
     [SCOTT *looks to see* MICHAEL *is staring at him and so are* JASON *and* RICK. SCOTT *moves away from* JASON *and remains apart from the group as* EMORY *bites loudly into a celery stalk. Everyone turns to stare at him.*]

HANK
     [*Continuing*]
Larry loved his students, and by God, he would go to class when he really didn't have the strength to even stand up. He taught when he was in such pain most of us would have...

DONALD
Begged for a morphine drip...

BERNARD
But Larry was clean and sober. Like Michael and me. We all wound up in different "rooms."

MICHAEL
[*Almost to himself*]
Ah, those rooms. Some dead, some dying.

BERNARD
[*Upbeat*]
But some saved.

HANK
[*Smiles to himself*]
My son said we needed God in the bullpen, but He was out of town with another team.

MICHAEL
What I don't understand about Christian Science is that you can have a million face-lifts, but you won't go to a doctor.

BERNARD
Larry never had a face-lift! Some people just look that good.

HANK
And he wasn't a Christian Scientist. He was a Scientologist.

DONALD
He *was*?

HANK
Well, for about five minutes.

BERNARD
He liked to try everything. I'm all for that.

EMORY
Remember when he was in EST? Once upon a time.
[*To JASON*]
I know you weren't born yet, so just cut me in half and count the rings.

BERNARD
[*Re drugs and booze*]
And he *Just Said No* up until he had to be taken to the hospital and then other people— doctors—started making the decisions.

RICK
[*Reflectively*]
I only met him after he was first hospitalized.

JASON
Did he ever come to terms with it?

BERNARD
Come to terms with what?

JASON
Being ashamed of what he had?

HANK
Ashamed?
[*A slight pause…*]

BERNARD
Larry didn't die of AIDS.

JASON
Well, I know that's the official story.

BERNARD
That's the *true* story! He died of *cancer*.

MICHAEL
Cancer without the "quotes." The respectable kind. The *esteemed*
kind. The kind you get where it doesn't show.

EMORY
Pancreatic.

RICK
Yeah, that's what was on his chart.

JASON
I thought it was…

MICHAEL
We know what you thought! Gay men *do* die of other things! They
do die of prostate tumors and heart attacks and get blown up on
planes and all the rest of those good things, just like real people!

EMORY
Or they're *murdered*.

MICHAEL

Or—they just die of old age. Their medical profiles are impeccable, but they're so old that when they pee sand comes out.

DONALD
          [*Absently*]
The thing about a real good heart attack is that it's fast.

EMORY

The good thing about Alzheimer's is that you get to hide your own Easter eggs.

BERNARD
What's good about *that?*

EMORY
Forget it.
          [*Realizes*]
Sorry!

HANK
What's good about cancer?

BERNARD
Nothing, except it's possible to beat it, and that's good.

EMORY
          [*Generally*]
You can get over a heart attack. Michael did.

JASON
          [*Sarcastically*]
You can't get over a *fatal* one.
          [*To EMORY*]
Are you sure Michael had a heart attack? Maybe it was just a pain down in his arm from the weight of his Rolex.

MICHAEL
You'll be happy to know I can't afford a Rolex and disappointed to hear I *do* have a heart.

JASON
It's only disappointing that you have such a *strong* one. You know, Michael, you may be the most cynical person I've ever encountered.

MICHAEL
Then they oughta let you out more often!

BERNARD
Please. Could we just…

MICHAEL
I see no reason for "*Forced Family Fun.*" Must we *pretend* to be
gay—and by that I mean in the linguistically traditional sense of the
word "gay"?!

JASON
That is the one thing you'll never have to pretend, in any sense.

EMORY
[*Privately amused, to JASON, coyly*]
Oh, you're *terrible*! But I like you.

JASON
[*Heated*]
I'm sick of self-centered retros like you, who wouldn't get their
Guccis stepped on, fighting for what they believe are—

HANK
[*Rises, the peacemaker*]
Now, wait a minute, fellas! This is not why we're here.

MICHAEL
I'm beginning to wonder why some of us *are* here.

RICK
You mean me.

MICHAEL
[*Bluntly, tolerantly*]
I *said* you were welcome!

JASON
[*To RICK*]
He means me. He's never liked me and never liked the fact that
Larry liked me.

MICHAEL
[*Testily*]
Doesn't anyone of this enlightened generation know how rude it is
to refer to someone in the third person who happens to be standing
in his presence?

JASON
You hate me and you hated my relationship with Larry—which was
none of your goddamn business.

MICHAEL
You didn't even know what he died of! What *relationship*?!

JASON
We were friends. Sometimes *loving* friends. At one time Larry and I
happened to be what he called "occasional regulars."
        [*HANK looks away.*]

RICK
Does that mean what I think it means?

JASON
It means what it means. I mostly bumped into him at Fire Island.

EMORY
Are people still going there?

JASON
You can't kill human nature. You can *die* of it, but you can't kill it.

EMORY
[*Placating JASON*]
I see nothing wrong with patrolling the lush, dark, tedious Pines—if
you play safe...

BERNARD
[*To EMORY, bluntly*]
You have hookers. That's hardly safe!

EMORY
I do not!

BERNARD
Bullshit. You don't know whether they're going to infect you or cut
your fucking throat.

160

JASON
When I saw him in the hospital, I was blown away. He'd been so hot...for an older guy.
[*To* MICHAEL]
So I made a mistake about what he died of! So, sue me!

MICHAEL
It's the city *you* ought to sue—for those legs.

JASON
What?

MICHAEL
You've got "sue the city legs." You ought to sue the city for building the sidewalk so close to your ass!

DONALD
[*To* MICHAEL]
You ought to keep your personality on a leash.

MICHAEL
You thought he'd been punished by God for his way of life!

JASON
That sounds more like something *you'd* think. I'm just sorry I jumped to a conclusion.

EMORY
If you're going to jump, you may as well dive. It gives a better line.

JASON
[*To* HANK]
I went to Larry's funeral *because* of the feeling I had for him.
[*To* MICHAEL]
And I'm *here* because of it. Throw me out if you want to! *You're* not my friend! Larry was! I'm here for *him*. And for myself.

BERNARD
If this is going to turn into something other than what it's meant to be, I'm going home. I've learned my lesson in this living room.

MICHAEL
Yeah, here we are back in the same old living room.

BERNARD
    [*Moving to leave*]
With the same old queens!

DONALD
Wait, Bernard…we're *all* upset.

EMORY
And you're all acting like kids!

HANK
    [*After a moment*]
Well, the grown-ups are acting like kids. The kids are acting quite
grown-up. Rick has barely opened his mouth. And Scott hasn't said
a word at all.
    [*SCOTT shifts uncomfortably, crosses to the bar cart to pick up a
    Diet Coke and go behind the stairs, his back to the group.*]

HANK
    [*Calmly*]
Look…we're here to share our sorrow, and we're free to act as angry
and frustrated and scared and sad and depressed as we feel.

MICHAEL
    [*Musically, "great star" largesse; lovely smile*]
And as "happy."
    [*For JASON's benefit*]
Or we're free to feel just as sad as if he *had* died of AIDS.

DONALD
    [*To MICHAEL*]
Why don't you have a double Shirley Temple and cool it.
    [*MICHAEL bristles at DONALD's remark. The door buzzes.*]

EMORY
Well, final*ment*!
    [*EMORY sits on the floor, behind the coffee table, leaning against the
    sofa. MICHAEL goes to press the door release button, opens the front
    door, goes out into the hallway.*]

HANK
Is it Harold?

MICHAEL
    [*Offstage*]
No. Flowers, I think.

JASON
Who needs a refill?
[*JASON goes to the bar cart, takes the Dom Perignon out of its cooler and goes to refill glasses—HANK's, EMORY's, RICK's. MICHAEL returns with a beautiful, elegantly arranged, home-grown cut flowers in a vase.*]

EMORY
[*Impressed*]
Oh, my, who sent that?!

MICHAEL
Do I know? They're for Hank.

EMORY
I can live without food, but I can't live without flowers.

BERNARD
Then you better lay off the chocolate-covered nasturtiums.
[*HANK opens the card.*]

HANK
[*Reads card*]
They're from Patsy and Jessica.

EMORY
The butch dykes who run the animal clinic?
[*Quickly corrects*]
The rather male-identified professional women in the country...?

RICK
[*To MICHAEL re flowers*]
Where're you going to put them?

EMORY
Well, Lady Astor always said, "Build a garden under a lamp." *And she oughta know.*
[*MICHAEL gives EMORY a look and plunks the bouquet in the middle of the coffee table, completely covering EMORY from view.*]

JASON
[*To EMORY*]
Don't you have any consciousness at all?

EMORY
[*Rising into view*]
I'm kidding, for Christ's sake!! That was a joke, you serious,
solemn sex machine! *Although,* I must tell you, dykes do not eat
egg salad sandwiches, and they don't pack their clothes in tissue
paper. *That* is a *vérité.*
[*BERNARD looks away. JASON shakes his head.*]

HANK
[*Ignoring everyone*]
I haven't been to the country for weeks, and Patsy and Jessica have
been so good about the dogs and the plants and the pipes—they've
really taken care of the place for us. Well, for me, now.

JASON
I don't know that gay men are going to be as supportive. Can you
see us marching for breast cancer?

DONALD
Yeah, we're not really interested in their culture—I mean, we don't
read lesbian novels or see the latest lesbian film, when it's almost a
supposition that they support gay men's art.

MICHAEL
Gay guys are so much more self-involved. They'll just continue
in their me-me-me, gym-gym-gym, sex-sex-sex, business-as-usual
way.

HANK
[*Continuing*]
Larry was only sixty. That's too young to die.

RICK
With all due respect, that's old to me. He seemed so much younger.

JASON
[*To HANK*]
Was he really sixty?

HANK
He knocked a few years off, but he was sixty. It was hard for him to
get old. He was the kind of guy who was meant to be young and
handsome forever.

MICHAEL

There's no such thing as fair—there's just luck. If I had to be born at all, I'd rather have been born male than female, rich rather than poor, straight instead of gay. It would have made life much easier *not* to have been gay.

[*Looks at* BERNARD]

And some of us got a double whammy, right, Bernard?

BERNARD

I'm surprised you didn't say, "Some of us got it in spades." If you want to hate, there's always something to hate about everybody.

MICHAEL

I'd rather be white instead of black, brown, yellow, or red. And that's just the way I feel. I'd rather be gentile than Jewish, Protestant rather than Catholic. Actually I'd rather have been religion-free...

[RICK, DONALD *react*]

It's *easier* that way.

DONALD

What's so great about the easy way out?

MICHAEL

Only a fool would want the *hard* way out. I'd rather be good-looking instead of plain—why couldn't we all truly have been created equal? It would have been just as easy, but, oh, no, that's not life. Some of us had to be born "interesting." And some of us, *not* so interesting. Some of us flat-out ugly. Some of us started out okay and wound up like toads. I want it easy! I want it all aces. I want something not so uphill as...life, *grinding, luckless life*!

JASON

You need help, Michael. Professional help. Your mind is like a bad neighborhood. You shouldn't go in there alone.

EMORY

[*To* JASON, *re* MICHAEL]

He's here, he's veneer, get used to it.

RICK

[*Crosses to the terrace doors, looks out*]

It's stopped raining.

DONALD
Yeah, why don't we all move outside on the terrace?

SCOTT
Good idea, it's getting pretty stale in here.

DONALD
Michael has sucked all the oxygen out of the air. That's about all
he's permitted to do these days.
[*MICHAEL ignores DONALD as JASON opens the doors.*]

MICHAEL
Emory just blew a fucking fortune fluffing it up for the summer.

EMORY
[*Gets up*]
I want to see if that hunky guy from the nursery did just what I told
him to do with the pots of geraniums.

JASON
I'd kill for a cigarette.

BERNARD
Me, too, but my wife and I finally gave it up. Booze first, then
tobacco.

JASON
Your wife?

HANK
[*Offhandedly*]
Things change.

BERNARD
She was my first sponsor.

JASON
You met her in a twelve-step program?

BERNARD
[*Nods*]
It was a slow process. We'd both been hurt—and dealt with it the
wrong way. So...we talked a long time, and then lived together a
long time, and then...I'm sorry she couldn't be here. She's in
Detroit with my mother, who's not well.

JASON
[*Curiously*]
She knows you're...well, whatever it is you are?

BERNARD
[*Smiles, nods*]
We know all about each other. She was married to a very nice, ordinary guy, but she says he treated her in a way that was...well, like what you might call "sexual bigotry"—although he didn't have a clue. He just behaved that way as a matter of course. With me, she says she feels like an equal. We have fun together.
[*With meaning*]
All kinds of fun.

JASON
Are you happy?

BERNARD
[*Drolly*]
You mean, in spite of my flying in the face of being gay and "going hetero"?

JASON
I'm just trying to understand.

BERNARD
Well, then...I guess I've come to think happiness is habit. And so, yeah. And, yeah, we love each other but, more important, we're each other's best friend. I used to not like sleeping with my friends—the people I laughed with and told everything to. But now, she's the only person I actually trust. And, oh, yeah, "the other" sometimes goes through my mind, but I've been there. And it didn't work out. I guess something could happen again, but I'm not planning on it.

EMORY
[*Quietly*]
But *I'm* your best friend.

BERNARD
[*Calmly, sincerely*]
No, I'm *your* best friend. You're my best *male* friend.
[*To JASON*]
I have to admit—it all scares the shit out of me.

JASON
Well, whatever works. Whatever does it for you. Whatever...*satisfies.*

EMORY
[*Sighs*]
Yeah. Like finding your own shade of rouge.
[*JASON removes a pack of cigarettes and goes outside.*]

RICK
I could stay in this room forever. This must be what they call soignée.

BERNARD
I think this child has been seduced by decor.

EMORY
[*With meaning*]
It wouldn't be the first time.
[*BERNARD gives EMORY a look as EMORY exits to terrace. RICK
wanders the room, studying things. The phone rings.*]

MICHAEL
[*Into phone*]
Hello? Yeah...oh, *hi*! Yeah, he's fine.

HANK
I bet that's my son.
[*RICK stops, looks up.*]

MICHAEL
[*Into phone*]
We'll see that he gets home. You both looked great too. Sorry you
can't drop by, but I understand. Let me know when the big day
arrives. Promise? Right. Bye.
[*Hangs up and says to HANK*]
It's too uncomfortable for Kate to get around till the baby comes.

DONALD
When's it due?

\HANK
Any minute.

BERNARD
Hank's second grandchild!

[*BERNARD crosses to check on* HANK *as* RICK *watches, curiously.* JASON *takes out a cigarette, puts it between his lips, and exits to the terrace, searching his pockets for matches.* HANK *drops his head and turns away.*]

EMORY
[*Loudly, offstage*]
That goddamn dumb, muscle-bound son-of-a-bitch from the nursery!! I told him no fucking vulgar Puerto Rican pink geraniums!! I said I only wanted pale Martha Washington colors!! But what did *he* know about *subtlety*!!
[HANK *dries his eyes, hands the handkerchief to* BERNARD...]

HANK
[*Re handkerchief*]
Thanks, Bernard.

BERNARD
That's yours, baby.
[BERNARD *takes the handkerchief and tucks it in* HANK's *suit breast pocket.*]

HANK
[*Nods*]
Oh, yeah, so it is. Thanks.

EMORY
[*Enters, almost in tears*]
This celebration of life is ruined! Just *ruined*!
[EMORY *whips back outside.* HANK *looks to see* RICK *staring at him. They exchange a smile.*]

DONALD
[*To* RICK, *flirting*]
I thought you wanted some air.

RICK
[*Forces a smile*]
I do. How about you?

DONALD
[*With a twinkle*]
Yeah, I'd love to come up for air.
[MICHAEL *takes stock of* DONALD *as he goes outside buzzing in* RICK's *ear.*]

EMORY
	[*Offstage, outraged*]
I...DON'T...FUCKING...BELIEVE IT!!!
	[MICHAEL *has crossed to the stairs and* SCOTT.]

MICHAEL
Champagne?

SCOTT
No, thank you.

MICHAEL
Not even for your birthday?

SCOTT
My birthday was two weeks ago.

MICHAEL
I know very well when your birthday was. Since we haven't spoken,
I was wondering how it went.

SCOTT
As you might expect, thanks to my father.

MICHAEL
And how *is* your father?

SCOTT
The same. After he asked me what I wanted for my birthday and I
told him, he didn't give me anything. Just blustered into my place
drunk; didn't even shake my hand.

MICHAEL
It seems that all you can really count on with him is for him to let
you down.
	[MICHAEL *puts his hand on* SCOTT's *shoulder as* DONALD *enters from
	the terrace.* SCOTT *sees* DONALD, *shrugs off* MICHAEL's *hand.*
	MICHAEL *looks at* DONALD.]

MICHAEL
	[*To* DONALD, *re* RICK]
How are you, shall we say, making out?

DONALD
	[*Re* SCOTT's *shrug*]
I'd say about the same as you. The chairs are wet.

170

MICHAEL
    [*With an edge*]
I'd say get some towels and dry them off.

DONALD
Right.
    [*Finishes his drink*]
First things first.
    [*DONALD goes to the bar cart and freshens his martini for* MICHAEL's
    benefit. MICHAEL *makes a disapproving face as* EMORY *flies inside.*]

EMORY
    [*Petulantly*]
What are we having to eat? I'm absolutely rav!

MICHAEL
Just some chicken hash and a little endive and watercress salad.
    [*RICK reenters.*]

EMORY
    [*Flirty, to* RICK]
Richarr, shall you and I heat up the Cuisine Duhzine?

RICK
Why don't I just wipe off the chairs. I'm better at cleaning up.
    [*Crestfallen,* EMORY *exits to the kitchen.* DONALD *crosses to the stairs,*
    drink in hand.]

DONALD
    [*To* MICHAEL, *with disgusted awe*]
Caterers and decorators.

MICHAEL
    [*Defensively*]
I just got a job!

DONALD
And you're already spending what you haven't made yet.

MICHAEL
    [*Dismissive*]
Yeah, yeah, yeah.

DONALD
I thought you told me you had to dip into your pension fund
because you hadn't worked in so long.

MICHAEL
I did. Anyone who doesn't live beyond his means suffers from a
lack of imagination!
    [*DONALD gives SCOTT a look, goes upstairs and into the bath.*]

SCOTT
    [*Re DONALD*]
He's jealous of me, isn't he?

MICHAEL
He's jealous of *me*. He just resents *you*.

SCOTT
Well, he doesn't have to feel threatened by *me*.
    [*MICHAEL is silent. SCOTT finishes his Diet Coke. MICHAEL turns to
    the group...*]

MICHAEL
    [*Graciously, but swallowing dryly*]
How're everybody's drinks?

HANK
    [*Hold up empty flute*]
Mind if I get a beer?

MICHAEL
Of course not. There's some in the fridge.
    [*HANK exits to the kitchen.*]

MICHAEL
    [*Sotto voce, to SCOTT*]
I was genuinely happy that you called this morning and suggested
we go to the service together. I wanted to see you before I left for
California.

SCOTT
Is it a good job?

MICHAEL
Just a TV rewrite.

SCOTT
How long will you be gone?

MICHAEL
A month or so.

172

SCOTT
[*After a moment*]
I'm so confused about our so-called friendship.

MICHAEL
Scott, I really don't think this is the proper time to get into all that.

SCOTT
Do I have to make an appointment?!
[*BERNARD and RICK look up. MICHAEL turns to them, smiles awkwardly. BERNARD takes a soft drink, opens it. MICHAEL turns away.*]

MICHAEL
No. You don't have to make an appointment.
[*After a moment*]
Why don't you go up to the bedroom, and I'll come up in a minute.

SCOTT
I think I'd just better leave.

MICHAEL
No, Scott, please, don't.

SCOTT
[*After a moment*]
I'm sorry I forgot to put the ice out.
[*DONALD comes downstairs to hear MICHAEL's plea. They exchange an uneasy look.*]

DONALD
[*Hands over towels*]
Here, Rick, start on the chairs, I'll get the cushions.
[*RICK exits to the terrace with the towels.*]

MICHAEL
[*Sotto voce, to SCOTT*]
Please? Go on. I'll be up in a minute.
[*SCOTT crushes his Diet Coke can, passes DONALD on the stairs, goes up, tearing off his T-shirt, continuing off into the bathroom. The bedroom light fades.*]

DONALD
[*Re SCOTT*]
It'll never work.

MICHAEL
Why?

DONALD
Because he doesn't make you laugh.

MICHAEL
[*Shaken, edgy*]
Something you read in a book? Or has the booze finally reached
what's left of your wet brain?
[*MICHAEL glares at DONALD, as EMORY exits the kitchen with a stack
of ceramic plates.*]

EMORY
[*Singsong*]
Behind you!
[*MICHAEL moves aside to let EMORY pass as JASON enters from the
terrace, exhaling from a discarded cigarette. He waves his hand to
disperse the smoke.*]

JASON
It's nice out.

EMORY
[*Whizzing past*]
Then *leave* it out!
[*EMORY exits to the terrace. In the bedroom SCOTT paces, sits on the
bed, then quickly gets up, smoothes the cover. Downstairs, DONALD
replenishes his drink.*]

MICHAEL
[*Not to DONALD*]
Will somebody roll the bar outside and get the wine while I see
about the food?

JASON
If you'll cease fire, I'll do the bar. I'm good at it, remember?

MICHAEL
[*Lightly, but unrelenting*]
You're sure you don't have a date on a float somewhere?
[*Sighs, to JASON*]
Okay...time out.
[*Indicates up right wall*]
The corkscrew and wine buckets are in the cabinet. The wine's in
the fridge.

174

[*JASON goes up right to an "invisible" cabinet: doors seamlessly cut into the photo blowup wall. He throws them open to reveal glass shelves that light up and contain a stupefying supply of liquor and glasses.*]

BERNARD
[*Reacts with anxious dismay*]
Good Christ, Michael!
[*MICHAEL remains completely cool...*]

MICHAEL
[*Sardonically*]
A fully stocked bar is a happy bar. Besides, these days you never know when there's going to be another celebration of life!
[*HANK enters from the kitchen with a bottle of beer in hand...*]

BERNARD
[*Unnerved, re bar*]
The sight of that is *staggering*—in the classic sense of the word!

MICHAEL
[*Facetiously*]
A sip is not a slip. Is it, Bernard?

BERNARD
[*Angrily*]
You're not serious!!

MICHAEL
Of course I'm not serious!

BERNARD
Who knows with you?

MICHAEL
[*Irritated*]
What do you mean by that?

BERNARD
I mean you still go to bars with people.

MICHAEL
I *accompany* people to bars. I happen to like the way bars smell.

175

BERNARD
And you drink nonalcoholic beer!

MICHAEL
It's less than five percent—less than what's in *orange juice*!

BERNARD
[*Re stocked hidden bar*]
And you keep this…this *speakeasy* behind closed doors!

MICHAEL
Speakeasy! You're dating yourself! I'm just not a zealot! And I should hardly think *you* would be!

BERNARD
After what we've been through?! It's like keeping a loaded gun in the apartment, just waiting for the baby to find it!

MICHAEL
Who the hell got you in the program in the first place, I'd like to know!

BERNARD
Well, now it looks like it's *my* turn! How much time have you got?

MICHAEL
Nine years!

BERNARD
Well, I slipped at *seven*! You're playing with fucking dynamite, man!

MICHAEL
Oh, Bernard, there's something comforting about having liquor on the premises. Like having prescription drugs. You just know they're there. I'd panic if there weren't any anesthetics in the house.

BERNARD
You sound like Harold.

HANK
Or Larry.

BERNARD
Fucking dynamite, man! Everything you say or do!

MICHAEL
I know, and I'm sorry! Did I upset you that much?

DONALD
Of course you upset him that much!

MICHAEL
Well, I apologize!

BERNARD
[*Levelly*]
It's all right to hate, Michael. It's just not all right to act in a hateful way.
[*BERNARD exits to the terrace, fuming.*]

MICHAEL
[*Re BERNARD's reaction*]
Christ of the Andes! Where did *that* come from?

DONALD
It wasn't funny.

MICHAEL
What about *you*! Still knocking them back as if time had stood still!
[*Re BERNARD*]
Why doesn't he say something to *you*?

DONALD
I *want* to drink, Michael.

MICHAEL
Well, so do I, but I can't because I'm a drunk!

DONALD
And so am *I* and so *what*?!
[*Drains his glass*]
Larry would have understood this conversation is out of bounds—why
can't you?!
[*MICHAEL restrains himself. JASON, having found the corkscrew and
a wine bucket, exits to kitchen. DONALD goes up right center to
another "invisible door," opens it, and removes some new, smartly
upholstered exterior chair cushions.*]

BERNARD
[*Offstage*]
Hey, Rick, my man, you really *do* know how to mop up!

RICK
[*Offstage*]
Well, I've cleaned enough toilets in my time.

BERNARD
[*Offstage*]
Yeah, what's one more or less, huh?
[*MICHAEL stiffens and exchanges a look with DONALD, who closes the
cabinet doors and exits to the terrace with the seat cushions.*

*HANK has gone to the étagère and put on a CD—something like Ella
Fitzgerald's "Skylark" begins to play. JASON enters with several
bottles of white wine, which he puts on the bar cart, then starts to
roll it outside. EMORY enters from the terrace as JASON starts to lift
the bar cart over the threshold...*]

EMORY
[*To JASON*]
Need a hand, big boy?

JASON
Thanks.

EMORY
I take it that you work out.

JASON
Yeah, American Fitness.

EMORY
[*Nods, knowingly, play-on-words*]
"Oh-Mary-Can-Ya-Lift-This"? The fit American goes to
American Fitness. That's why Eighth Avenue between
Fourteenth and Twenty-third looks like an open call for
Spartacus, the Musical.
[*They lift the bar cart over the jamb and exit to the terrace.
MICHAEL sees HANK has picked up a photograph in a silver frame
on the étagère and is looking at it. MICHAEL comes over to HANK...*]

HANK
[*Re SCOTT's photo*]
He's a handsome kid, Michael.

MICHAEL
Scott's aunt took that of us.

HANK
He introduced you to his family?

MICHAEL
He just wanted me to meet his aunt. She's all he cares about—the only one who's ever been the least bit kind to him. We took her to lunch. I loaned Scott my dark blue cashmere blazer, and he looked so elegant. His aunt was so proud of him. She held his hand on the top of the table for a long time after the plates had been cleared away, and he didn't seem uncomfortable at all.

HANK
Is he uncomfortable at a show of affection?

MICHAEL
From some people, I guess.

HANK
He looks *very* proud of you, Michael.
[*MICHAEL smiles, takes the picture of SCOTT from HANK, turns, and goes up the stairs.*

HANK now picks up a photograph of Larry and studies it a moment. DONALD and RICK come inside. RICK watches HANK.]

DONALD
[*To HANK*]
Nice shot of Larry.

HANK
I think so. Brazil was great. We had a good time there.
[*HANK replaces the photograph and exits to the terrace. RICK goes to the étagère, picks up the framed photograph of Larry. Suddenly, RICK dissolves into tears. DONALD goes to him, puts his arm around him.*]

RICK
[*Distraught*]
Oh, God, Donald, what am I going to do?!

DONALD
What you can't do is let Hank see you break down.

RICK
[*Sobbing*]
I loved him.

DONALD
I know you did. Sort of like the hostage-captor syndrome in reverse, I guess.

RICK

Please, don't joke! I helped him die. He begged me to turn up the drip till he was gone, then turn it down before I called the doctor. I *couldn't*. I…I…put some morphine suppositories on his bedside table, then I left the room. When I came back, I took the empty foil wrappers and flushed them down the toilet so no one would know. Then, I did what he told me. I called the doctor.

> [*RICK falls against DONALD and sobs. DONALD puts his arms about RICK, kisses him on his cheek, forehead, and, finally, sweetly on the mouth. RICK responds passionately. JASON enters with the empty ice bucket, stops on a dime, watches them. RICK's head goes limp on DONALD's shoulder.*]

RICK

I wonder who else knows I loved him?

DONALD

I don't think anyone *here* knows…

> [*Looks up at JASON*]

Well…

JASON

I don't know a thing. Not a thing.

RICK

> [*Recovering*]

There's nothing to know, really, except that I…felt about Larry the way I do. I think he just liked the idea that I was crazy about him.

> [*To DONALD*]

You never told Michael, did you?

DONALD

Of course not.

> [*JASON turns and exits to the kitchen.*]

RICK

> [*Looks at photo of Larry*]

He was so much fun. When he was in remission, after his classes, we had kind of a standing date. Nothing much, really—Starbuck's, the movies, my place. He was so loving.

> [*Through tears*]

But I knew it could never lead to anything.

> [*RICK puts the photo back on the shelf.*]

Hank never knew. He hardly remembers me. I'm sorry about this…acting like this…

DONALD
I understand.

RICK
Thanks, Donald. I hope you don't get the wrong idea.

DONALD
What's a little kiss between friends?
[*They get a grip. JASON enters, the ice bucket refilled.*]

RICK
Have you seen my guitar case?

JASON
[*Nods*]
In the kitchen. You gonna sing us that song?

RICK
I'm gonna sing somebody that song.
[*RICK exits to the kitchen.*]

JASON
So, Bernard says you live in the Hamptons. I'm house-sitting for a friend out there.

DONALD
Well, you ought to give me a call. We could have a picnic on the beach…

JASON
It's still a little chilly for that, isn't it?

DONALD
I could make a thermos of martinis.

JASON
I'm in the program.

DONALD
Not you too! You're like the pod people!

JASON
[*Laughs*]
There's only Michael and Bernard and me left. Three out of nine—that's not such a frightening average. And a bartender!

DONALD
Keep up the good work!

JASON
I feel like such an enabler. You know, what's wrong with this
picture?!

DONALD
I'll give you my phone number anyway.
[*DONALD and JASON go outside onto the terrace in conversation.
Lights begin to fade as RICK exits the kitchen with his guitar. He
strums a few chords, goes onto the terrace.*

*Lights fade out downstairs, come up in the bedroom as SCOTT exits
the bath, pulling on one of MICHAEL's solid cashmere sweaters. He
sees MICHAEL put down the photograph of them.*]

SCOTT
My T-shirt was damp. Mind if I borrow this?
[*MICHAEL shakes his head*]
You cleaned out the medicine cabinet.

MICHAEL
I didn't. Maybe the maid did. Looking for something?

SCOTT
I kinda got a headache.
[*After an awkward pause...*]
Listen, I quit school.

MICHAEL
I know. I was wondering if you were going to tell me.

SCOTT
How do you know? Did one of those old bastards...

MICHAEL
No, I went to meet you after class last week. I thought we ought to
have a chat and clear the air. You weren't there.

SCOTT
NYU was a mistake. I was in over my head. I couldn't cut it.

MICHAEL
It's my fault for insisting.

182

SCOTT

No, it's not. I like it that you cared. It's more than my own father
ever did. I think I need to work outdoors. Landscape gardening. Or
maybe I could be a vet. Maybe you could introduce me to those
friends of Hank's in the Hamptons.

MICHAEL

Sure. Anything. But, Scott, *study something*. You've got a good mind.

SCOTT

Listen, I think I'm going to slip out now. You know, parties—well,
whatever you call this—are just not my thing.
   [*MICHAEL nods.*]

SCOTT

Now I suppose you're going to drop the bomb.

MICHAEL
   [*After a moment*]
I'm simply going to try to tell you how I feel. Unless there is
some physical contact, some show of...affection...between us...I
can't...

SCOTT

Here it comes.

MICHAEL

What does "drop the bomb" really mean?

SCOTT

What do you think?

MICHAEL

Well...I think you think that it means you will be emotionally
betrayed. *Abandoned*—which seems to be the major theme of your life.

SCOTT

Michael, just say what's on your mind and I'll go.

MICHAEL

I've said it.

SCOTT
   [*Sheepishly*]
You want me to go now?

MICHAEL
      [*Sharply*]
Scott, *make sense*! You knew from the start how I felt about you!

SCOTT
Knew what *you* wanted, you mean!

MICHAEL
Yes! I've never tried to hide what I wanted. And in spite of the
"threat" to you, you allowed things to progress.

SCOTT
Threat?

MICHAEL
      [*Impatiently*]
You heard me. *Threat.* A show of those feelings from me, a negative
response from you, and my reaction—which to you meant that I
would go away and leave you.
      [*SCOTT goes to sit on the bed, but the moment he does he gets up and
      moves to a chair.*]

SCOTT
I don't want any emotional involvement with anyone! Or physical,
either! I like you as a friend. Why can't we leave it at that?

MICHAEL
Scott, I don't want to continue in what is a painful and unhappy
situation for me. But you don't want to hear that. Because you
want all the advantages and none of the responsibilities. In short,
you want me to be a checkbook and an ear. Well, what's in this
for *me*?!
      [*SCOTT gets up, picks up the picture, looks at it.*]

SCOTT
I don't want things to change. In any way. I've told you that
my aversion to being touched is not just with you, it's with everybody.

MICHAEL
That's not good enough! Scott, we were like lovers without the sex.

SCOTT
My body is my own.

184

MICHAEL
[*Coolly*]
Well, yes. It is. Yours to keep or to give to whomever you want. And if you don't want to give yourself to me, you must try to understand what that does to me!

SCOTT
Do I have to try in front of all these old farts?!

MICHAEL
I suppose you mean my contemporaries. And of course, I'm folklore.

SCOTT
I'm sorry. I actually like them. Well, *two* of them. —Well...*one* of them.

MICHAEL
Chronologically, I am aware that I could be your father. In some climates, possibly your grandfather.

SCOTT
Age has nothing to do with it. *Really.*
[*Frustrated*]
Oh, forget it. Goodbye.
[*SCOTT makes a move toward the stairs, MICHAEL doesn't try to stop him. SCOTT stops, says emphatically...*]
I said, *goodbye.*

MICHAEL
[*As if he's just heard him. Casually*]
Sorry. Goodbye.

[*SCOTT is silent, sinks to the floor, starts to weep. MICHAEL looks at him for a moment, then goes to lower himself to the floor beside him.*]

SCOTT
It has nothing to do with *you*, I've told you that. It's with anybody. *I don't want to be touched!*

MICHAEL
[*Touches SCOTT's knee*]
Are you really that damaged?
[*SCOTT recoils*]
Or am I repulsive to you? Tell me. I can take it. It would be such a relief to know what's really going on in your head.

SCOTT
[*Turns away, sobs uncontrollably*]
I can't fight the things that have been done to me.

MICHAEL
Listen, my roots were, I think, uglier than your own—an emotional
torment I don't know how I survived.

SCOTT
[*Weeping*]
How'd you do it?

MICHAEL
I met people who were smarter and wiser than I was, and I learned
from them. Like I've tried to pass on things to you.
[*Directly*]
Like believing in yourself. Your *self*: that thing you feel when you
go through a revolving door—that post, that center, that something
unshakable...around which everything else spins!
[*SCOTT turns to MICHAEL, keeping his distance...*]

SCOTT
[*Through tears*]
I had always hoped...dreamed that one day I would somehow cross
paths with a person like you—someone who'd see something in me.
Don't you think I know you've spent a lot of money on me—all the
restaurants and clothes and the classes you've paid for? And don't
you know I can't help feeling, in some way, undeserving of all this?
[*SCOTT starts to dry his eyes, gets to his feet...*]
But I know it'll payoff, though I could never pay you back.
[*MICHAEL stands up next to SCOTT.*]

MICHAEL
[*With meaning*]
Yes, you could.
[*MICHAEL turns back, embraces SCOTT awkwardly. SCOTT is thrown,
flustered.*]

SCOTT
[*Jokey, laughing nervously*]
Quick! Fast-forward this! Michael hangs on to him steadfastly...

MICHAEL
[*Intense whisper*]
Be *real*!

[*SCOTT violently disentangles himself, stumbles backward awkwardly, flailing his arms, panicked. He almost falls over a chair, almost upsets the bedside table. MICHAEL doesn't move, straightens with a regained dignity. SCOTT recovers, stumbles downstairs, stops in the middle of the room, leans against the sofa, gasping for air. MICHAEL slowly descends the stairs.*]

MICHAEL
[*Looks at SCOTT*]
Breathe! You always stop breathing the moment there's any inference of emotion or sexual demand...

SCOTT
[*Hyperventilating*]
I can't!

MICHAEL
Take a breath, goddamn it!

SCOTT
[*Gets up, gets his breath*]
I can't help it if I feel like...like I'm suffocating.

MICHAEL
Well, I wanted many things—but never to *asphyxiate* you. I want you to be able to feel something authentic for someone. If not me, then someone else. Even if you have to abandon *me*.

SCOTT
[*Not looking at MICHAEL*]
When I was seventeen I was already getting into bars with a fake ID...this guy came on to me—but the more he did, the more I was obnoxious.

SCOTT
I don't know when he left the bar, but I stayed till it closed and started walking home. At a traffic light a car pulled up beside me. It was the guy. He offered me a ride. I knew it was stupid, but I got in. He pulled a gun and drove me all the way to his place in Jersey.

MICHAEL
[*Quietly*]
Oh, Christ.

SCOTT
[*Takes a breath*]
He ordered me into his house and handcuffed me at gunpoint. He made me take my clothes off, then he shot me up on drugs and loaded a pistol. Then he blindfolded me and fucked me with the barrel.
[*Turns to* MICHAEL]
I was so drugged, so scared that it became a sort of "out of body" experience. When it was over, he uncuffed me and handed me the gun and told me to shoot him for what he'd done.

MICHAEL
Well, I certainly hope you *did*.

SCOTT
[*Shakes his head*]
He tried to make me take money to make up for it. And I refused. Finally, he offered me drugs. And even though I really wanted them, I refused. I pulled on my clothes the best I could and staggered out and just kept trying to put one foot in front of the other.
[*After a moment*]
Did you know that Emory is working on some very "rah-sha-sha" needlepoint pillow that says "Elegance Is Refusal"?

MICHAEL
[*Nods sardonically at the "in" joke, re "recherché"*]
Yes, *very* "rah-sha-sha."
[*They both break-up laughing*]

SCOTT
[*Comes closer to* MICHAEL, *reflectively*]
I was the way I am before that ever happened. I'd had sex before then. I just never liked it all that much. It was never possible for me to combine being physical with someone who I'd let into my confidence.

MICHAEL
Are you trying to tell me that's why I have the rare privilege of your body *language* rather than your *body*?

SCOTT
[*Comes closer*]
It's the way I am. I'm as queer as I can be and have no problem with that, but I don't like to be touched. I don't like to be stared at. I won't even shower at the gym after my workout.

MICHAEL
Why, is it too cruisy?

SCOTT
    [*Tough*]
Life is cruisy!

MICHAEL
    [*After a moment*]
I love you.

SCOTT
    [*After a moment*]
And I love you too.

MICHAEL
Well, I guess sometimes love just isn't enough.
    [SCOTT *is silent, gets his bicycle, rolls it to the front door…*]

MICHAEL
You think Jason had a point? You think maybe it was one of your
friends who took your bike?

SCOTT
I never have anyone over. You know that. I must have just left my
door unlocked by mistake.
    [*Starts to move, stops…*]
Uh, I hate to ask you this, but can I borrow twenty dollars?
    [MICHAEL *takes his wallet out of his pocket without hesitation, gives
    it to him.*]

MICHAEL
Here—take forty. Or sixty. Take whatever you want.

SCOTT
Forty's enough.
    [SCOTT *hands the wallet back to* MICHAEL, *who returns it to his pocket.*]

SCOTT
Thanks.
    [*Unyielding eye contact*]
I'll never forget what you've gone through with me, and I'm going
to try to make sure the effort wasn't for nothing.

MICHAEL
    [*Simply*]
Thanks.

SCOTT

I'm sad that I haven't turned out to be what you'd hoped I'd be for you. I'm sad that I still don't know how to love or be loved.

MICHAEL

I hope you find out before you're my age.

[*SCOTT opens the front door, rolls the bike out, and closes the door. MICHAEL doesn't move. HANK has entered in time to see SCOTT exit, but SCOTT does not see him. MICHAEL turns.*]

HANK

Doesn't Scott want anything to eat before he goes?

MICHAEL

[*After a moment*]

It's not going to work out, Hank. I think he's gone for good.

HANK

Did he tell you that?

MICHAEL

He didn't have to.

HANK

Are you okay?

MICHAEL

Let's see...what am I? Crushed. Depressed. Suicidal. No, not that. I've always looked for love in inappropriate places. So, yeah, I'm okay. I'm fine. I won't drink over this, if that's what you mean.

HANK

That's what I mean.

MICHAEL

To be honest, I want to, but if I did I might as well put a gun to my head. Not that that wouldn't be a welcome relief. Anyway, I don't want that. Not *yet,* anyway. So...not to worry. Hank, I'm that dreaded word...*survivor.*

HANK

Michael—the love of another person is a discipline not easily won or maintained.

MICHAEL
But you think it's worth the risk.

HANK
It took a long time for Larry and me to get to that point. Well, that is, it took *me* a long time. But I finally understood what he was driving at. It's so simple. You be you. I'll be me. *But...*we'll be together.
[*The doorbell rings three times.* MICHAEL *looks at* HANK *expectantly, goes to the door, and opens it.* HAROLD *is standing there, not having aged a great deal; still thin, still with kinky black hair. He has on sunglasses and a rain cape and carries a dripping umbrella.*]

MICHAEL
Well, if it isn't the antichrist!

HAROLD
I take it you were expecting someone else. I rang thrice so you wouldn't think it was the postman and get all wet and coozy.

MICHAEL
How'd you get in?

HAROLD
Your divine super was mopping up downstairs. Feisty little bugger. I told him I was here for the Yale reunion. He directed me to your apartment.
[*He hands his umbrella to* MICHAEL, *slips out of his rain cape, and hands that to* MICHAEL *too, as if he were an attendant.*]

BERNARD
[*Enters from terrace*]
What've you been doing with that blond, Harold?

HAROLD
[*Kissing* BERNARD]
Petal!

BERNARD
You're so tanned!

HAROLD
I've been in St. Bart's—playing Dorothy Dandridge in *Island in the Sun.*

MICHAEL
Everybody else came directly from the service! That was an hour
ago, at the very least!
 [*Dumps umbrella and cape*]
There's been time for a deluge! Foyers have been flooded! Arks
have been built!

HAROLD
 [*Entering*]
Surely you know by now I have absolutely no sense of time.

MICHAEL
If that is true, then why are you never an hour *early*?!

BERNARD
Maybe your watch stopped.

HAROLD
 [*Looks at his watch*]
I don't think so. It was running perfectly when my man put it on
me this morning.
 [*Reacting to light*]
Oh, my *God*, this is real straight-boy lighting! What *is* this, the open-
heart surgery room?!

MICHAEL
You're stoned!
 [*EMORY pops in from the kitchen with a silver casserole in chafing
 frame.*]

HAROLD
Hello, d'yah.
 [*NOTE: That's "dear" very, very clipped.*]

EMORY
You're just in time for food, Hallie.

HAROLD
Oh-I-can't-eat-a-thing-what-are-you-having?

EMORY
Lean and mean "Cuisine Duhzine."

192

HAROLD
[*For MICHAEL's benefit*]
Ohh, minced pig's nipples on toast points. From that trendy frog
gonif on Second Avenue?
[*EMORY hoots, whips outside as DONALD enters. HAROLD passes
DONALD en route to HANK.*]

HAROLD
[*Not looking at him and not stopping*]
Donald, good to see you.

DONALD
[*With resignation*]
As always, Harold.
[*DONALD goes to the wall bar, removes a stack of Italian ceramic
plates. HAROLD comes up to HANK, takes his hands.*]

HAROLD
[*With great feeling*]
Hank. How are you, bubelah?

HANK
[*Hugs HAROLD*]
Thanks for everything, Harold. I couldn't have arranged it without
your help.

HAROLD
What can I tell you, some of my best friends are morticians.
[*Sincerely*]
I wish I could say I know just how you feel. I have no idea how
you feel. That was a terrific little mention in the *Post* on Larry's
work.

HANK
I thought so.

EMORY
[*Enters, empty-handed*]
Oh, I didn't see it, and I read the *Post* every day.

HAROLD
It was in the Lifestyle section. We're never news—we're always
lifestyles.
[*Outside, RICK begins to strum his guitar.*]

EMORY

Oh, Rick's about to sing! I'd better get my act together.
> [EMORY *runs up the stairs and into the bath, closing the door.*
> *Meanwhile,* HAROLD *goes to the terrace door, looks outside.*]

HAROLD
> [*Re group on terrace*]

Jesus! It looks like the United Colors of Benetton out there!
> [*To* MICHAEL]

Have you got Sitting Bull stashed in the closet?

HANK

Some of Larry's younger friends.

HAROLD

And a fine looking lot they are too. The white one's a serial killer, at
the very least. And I thoroughly approve of him.

MICHAEL

Who was the bottle blond you were with at the service?

HAROLD

An actor-singer-dancer-waiter. Well, he's not really a dancer,
but he moves. In fact he's moving into my apartment this very
minute.

MICHAEL

What?!!

HAROLD

Just temporarily till he finds a place. I'm only trying to do my bit for
the arts. He sent his regrets.

MICHAEL

I'm *distraught* that he couldn't come.

HAROLD

I knew you would be. He and I are making dinner at home tonight
so I dare not eat a thing. In fact, I've got to lose twenty pounds by
seven-thirty. He's cute as a mouse's ear, dontcha think?
> [*Exits to terrace, expansively.*]

Hello, boys, here's your Aunt Harold! Come cheer me up!
> [*He glides outside, humming. Those left in his wake exchange looks.*
> RICK *can be heard singing "Que Reste-il De Nos Amours? (What's*
> *Left of Our Love?)" French lyrics and music by Charles Trenet.*
> *(NOTE: The English version is called "I Wish You Love," and the*

*lyrics, like the title, by Albert A. Beach are original, not an adapted
translation of Trenet.) The stage lights begin to fade…*]

RICK
[*Offstage; sings*]
*Ce soir, le vent qui frappe a ma porte
Me parle des amours morts
Devant le feu qui s'éteint.*

*Ce soir, c'est une chanson d'automne
Dans la maison qui frissonne
Où je pense aux jours lointains…*

[*MICHAEL is left alone, moves toward the bar cabinet. He opens it.
In the fading light, it seems even brighter, more sparkling, more
seductive than before. RICK's voice continues outside…*]

RICK
[*Offstage, singing*]
*Que reste-il de nos amours?
Que reste-il de ces beaux jours?
Une photo, une vieille photo
De ma jeunesse….*

[*The lights fade, with only the bar light intensifying. Another
moment…*]

B L A C K O U T

E N D   O F   A C T   1

A c t 2

As the house lights fade, Rick's voice can be heard signing, accompanying himself on the guitar...

RICK
[*Offstage, singing*]
Les mots, les mots tendres qu'on murmure
Les caresses les plus pures
Les sermons au fond d'un tiroir

Les fleurs, qu'on retrouve dans un livre
Dont le parfum vous enivre / Se sont envoles, pourquoi?

Que reste-il des billets doux
Du mois d'Avril, des rendezvous
Un souvenir que me poursuit
Sans cesse.

[*As the lights come up on stage,* MICHAEL *closes the bar cabinet, shutting off its light. Outside, on the terrace,* RICK *finishes up Que Reste-il De Nos Amours.*]

RICK
[*Offstage, singing*]
Bonheur fane
Cheveux au vent
Baisers voles
Rêves émouvants
Que reste-il de tout cela?
Dites-le moi.

Un p'tit village, un viêux clocher
Un paysage si bien caché
Et dans un nuage le cher visage
De mon passé.

[*Applause from all.* MICHAEL *slowly crosses to the terrace door.*]

HAROLD
[*Offstage*]
Fabulous, Rickola! Or, should I say, "Fah-boo-*luzz*"! Now, let's hear a *Yankee* song! For us *Yanks*!

MICHAEL
[*At terrace door*]
That *was* a Yankee song, Harold! For us Yanks from New Orleans.
[*Thunder. Groans all around from everyone outside.*]

HAROLD
[*Offstage, in comic Southern accent*]
Well, ah declare, y'all, ah do believe we are about to have a spring *squall*!

BERNARD
[*Offstage, in comic Southern accent*]
Sugah, you know a real good squallin' generally follows a heat wave—'specially a *French* one!
[*There is a clap of thunder. Audible reactions from the group outside, followed by the sound of a sudden downpour.*]

MICHAEL
Just leave everything on the table under the awning and cover the casserole!
[*Much hooting as everyone dashes inside, most carrying their drinks, plates of food, and smart cotton napkins, which they use to blot the raindrops. RICK hangs on to his guitar but waves an empty stem glass...*]

RICK
Did anyone grab that champagne?

DONALD
[*Holding up Bombay bottle*]
I grabbed the champagne of bottled gins. First things first!

MICHAEL
[*To DONALD, disapprovingly*]
You *could* just start the day with a gin enema. Why fuck around and wait for things to take effect?
[*To RICK, re champagne*]
There's a bottle of Cristal in the fridge.
[*Re rainstorm*]
Somebody close the doors till it slackens a bit!

HAROLD
[*Blotting his brow*]
Maybe we ought to ask the super to come up and mop us off.
[*JASON slides the terrace doors shut. RICK goes to put his guitar back in its case.*]

JASON
[*To RICK*]
Rick, what's that song mean in plain English?

BERNARD
Yeah, what about us dumb bastards who didn't go to Le Rosey?
[*RICK strums the intro again and speaks the song in a loose translation of the original French, not the Albert A. Beach English lyrics of "I Wish You Love." RICK accompanies his oral recitation (delivered more briskly than the singing) with the appropriate chords...*]

RICK
[*Speaking, not singing*]
Tonight, the wind that beats on my door
Speaks to me of love that's lost
And I think of times gone by...

What is there left of our love?
What is there left of happy days?
A photograph, an old photo
Of my youth...

Of faded bliss,
Of wind-blown hair?
A stolen kiss,
A dream we share—
What's left of this?
Can you tell me?
A memory.

Letters you wrote that I still keep
Lines I can quote that make me weep
The rest is gone. Why is it gone?
Pourquoi?

[*More enthusiastic applause than before.*]

MICHAEL
[*To* BERNARD]
You *do* comprehend "pourquoi," don't you?

BERNARD
Yeah, it means "fuck *you*," doesn't it?
[*HANK crosses to* RICK.]

HANK
[*Calmly, sincerely*]
That was terrific, Rick. Really. Larry told you he liked that song?

RICK
[*Carefully*]
Yeah.
[*Deeply appreciative*]
I'm glad *you* liked it, Hank. I hoped you would.

HANK
I did. Very, very much. Thank you.
[*RICK smiles at* HANK, *turns to go put his guitar in its case.*]

BERNARD
[*Looking about*]
Where the hell is Emory?

HAROLD
Who's next on the bill and what language is it in?
[*The bathroom door opens,* EMORY *quickly emerges and strikes a pose at the top of the stairs.*]

EMORY
[*Theatrically*]
I'm next! And it's in the mother tongue! For all you *mothers*!
[*Everyone looks up as a kind of vision descends the stairs.* EMORY *is completely (and wonderfully) made up: bright, glossy red lipstick, shaded cheekbones, dramatic eye shadow, and thick false lashes. No wig, however, and no women's clothes. He has only put on the jacket to his black velour suit, turned up the lapels, and buttoned it to the throat. Around his neck are several strands of sparkling rhinestones. Brilliant drops dangle from his ears, and on his wrists and fingers are dazzling bracelets and rings. (He is carrying a cassette and a small camera.)*]

[*Instant applause, hoots, and whistles.*]

200

[*EMORY goes to pop the cassette into the tape deck and deposit his camera on the étagère. There is a round of applause as everyone settles into chairs, on the stairs, or on the floor.*]

EMORY
    [*A seasoned pro from the school of yesteryear*]
Thank you. Thank you, ladies and gentlemen—and you among you know who's who. This next little ditty does not come from Paris, or Pa*ree*, whichever you prefer. —Personally, I prefer New York! Yes, make mine Manhattan, and make my day!
    [*Imperiously, to MICHAEL*]
Michael, my *lights*! My *lights*!
    [*MICHAEL goes to a wall switch as the intro on the tape begins. A hush falls over the, room, MICHAEL hits the wall switch, and EMORY stands in a lone pool of strategically focused light.*]
    [*The next exchanges are rapid volleys…*]

HAROLD
Oh, the Marlene keylight! Why didn't I have that for my entrance?!

EMORY
Check the cheekbones!

BERNARD
Did you say chicken bones?

EMORY
    [*Re BERNARD*]
Oh, *kill her*! *Cheek*bones! How're my cheekbones?

JASON
They look like Carlsbad Caverns!

EMORY
    [*Playfully*]
Well, that's not because of the light. That's because I had all my wisdom teeth extracted this afternoon!
    [*He sucks in his cheeks. Mild laughter.*]

EMORY
    [*Campily sultry*]
I come before you without wisdom.
    [*French pronunciation*]
But with "cou*rage*."

HAROLD
Yeah, first comes "cou*rage*," then comes regret.

EMORY
[*American accent*]
Je ne regrette rien, cheri!
    [BERNARD *sits on the stairs, gives a grandstand razz...*]

BERNARD
[*Through cupped hands*]
I hope your song's better'n your material!

EMORY
[*To* BERNARD]
Oh, you're *terrible*!

BERNARD
But you're fucking nuts about me!

DONALD
[*To* BERNARD]
Quiet in the bleachers!

JASON
Yeah, come on, guys, settle down! Shhh...
    [*Everyone quiets.* EMORY *stands perfectly still in his "spotlight,"
    sparkling with command.*]

EMORY
[*Over accompaniment*]
Larry always spoke up for freedom. Freedom to be yourself, with
no need to lie or pretend. This song is for Larry.
    [*The taped intro ends, and the accompaniment begins. Emory
    sings/speaks a song entitled "I'm Not the Man I Planned." NOTE:
    What follows is a suggestion of what the "flavor" ought to be—
    particularly its bawdy music hall/burlesque house tone.*]

EMORY
[*Sings/speaks*]
I'm not the man I planned:
A life I'd founded on fam'ly aesthetics,
A wife surrounded with kids and athletics.
Instead I astounded the town with cosmetics.
My structure faltered—
My foundation altered—
An' I'm not the man I planned.

EMORY [*Cont'd*]
I'm not the guy I dreamed.
The square in conventional coats and ties.
Though I still wear suits, now I mesmerize
Simply because I accessorize.
>   [*He whips a red ostrich fan from under his jacket, snaps it open, and fans himself.*]

With plumage I pepped up
With high high heels I schlepped up
And I'm not the guy I dreamed!
Now it's a cinch,
I'm gay as a finch!
And I tell you without much ado—
I'm such a queer *bird*
That maybe you've *heard*
I'd never love a dove
But I'd kiss a cockatoo!
>   [*Singing*]

I'm no longer boring and bland,
A dead-on-arrival fashion victim
Now I'm archival, and this is my dictum:
Provincial drag is an outmoded mess.
Come to New York 'n' cross-dress for success
I divested in transis.
Got arrested in Kansas…
But I shout "Eureka and encore!
I'm not in Topeka anymore!"
And thank God not the clod I planned.
>   [*Applause and whistles.* EMORY *bows graciously, a geisha shielding half his face behind his fan. The noise dies down…*]

MICHAEL
How many musical interludes are there going to be?

HAROLD
Well, I hope it's not like what they used to say about films from India: "If it's serious, there are only *ten* numbers." Just kidding, Em, you were heaven!

EMORY
>   [*To* HAROLD]

That was the second and *last* number, thank you very much! I always close the bill! The musical portion, anyhow.

MICHAEL
[*To the group*]
Now, anybody who has something to say can say it.
[*There is some low mumbling among the group, but no one stands immediately...*]

EMORY
[*Low hiss*]
Bernard! Bernard! Say something!
[*EMORY crosses to the étagère to put away his fan and get his camera. BERNARD stands, clears his throat as EMORY goes to sit on the stairs unobtrusively.*]

BERNARD
[*To the group*]
The last time I went to see Larry in the hospital he said a funny thing to me—because no matter what spiritual fad he was into, he really thought organized religion was destructive and just caused trouble between people. So I was surprised when he said, "After I'm gone, will you do me a favor? Will you go in a church and light a candle for me?" And of course, I didn't question him, I just said I would. But then in typical Larry fashion he added: "Not just *any* old church but someplace like that one you see across the street when you come out of the 50th Street side door of Sak's 5th Avenue." That was Larry.
[*Applause. BERNARD sits down as HAROLD goes to the étagère and picks up the photograph of Larry...*]

HAROLD
Has everybody seen this wonderful picture of Lar? Hank took it on the beach in Brazil.
[*HAROLD hands it to the person nearest him and it is passed hand-to-hand in a circle until it is seen by all and returned to him. Meanwhile...*]

HAROLD
[*To HANK*]
How long ago?

HANK
I swear I can't remember.

JASON
[*Coolly*]
It'll be three years this summer.

RICK
That's a great straw hat. He had style.

EMORY
In fact, sometimes he was style-*heavy*. Remember the summer
when he bought fish bowls from Pier 1 for wineglasses?

DONALD
[*Nostalgically*]
And we never had to get up to freshen our drinks.

BERNARD
And when we *had* to get up, we *couldn't*!
[*Laughter from the old-timers, especially* DONALD. RICK *and* JASON
don't find it funny, and BERNARD's *smile fades with realization…*]

BERNARD
Gives me the shakes just thinking about it.

MICHAEL
[*Absently*]
Me too.

EMORY
[*To* RICK]
That was back when we smoked and drank and there were no gyms
and restaurants cooked with grease.

HAROLD
Yeah, and the baths were great for emergency love.

MICHAEL
Yeah, and I hated myself for being gay. Then I came out, and *other*
people hated me.

JASON
The dark ages.
[*Laughter.*]

EMORY
Yeah. Now the world's enlightened and in a holding pattern. I'm in
a holding pattern. Well, I know my *looks* are in a holding pattern.
Now, who's gonna say something?
[*There is a moment of mumbling as everyone wonders who's going
to be the next person to speak.* JASON *stands and the group quiets as*
HAROLD *replaces the picture on the* étagère…]

JASON
[*To the group*]
It was not in Larry's nature to be somber or self-pitying, so I'm
going to do my best to be like him. We, in this room, are Larry's
"family." Each of us was sort of a different relative, with a different
sort of relationship. Each of us may know something about him the
others do not, but each of us knows what the other has lost. I think
it's his honesty I'll remember most—more than his wit or his charm
or his ageless good looks.
[*A round of applause*]

[*Shifting gears*]
Larry loved life and lived it by his own code. There was an edge to
everything he believed or said, whether it was smart-ass or serious.
He had his own standards and refused to live by...

MICHAEL
Where's this going?

JASON
Larry believed that men with men—and women with women—are
a completely different human dynamic from men with women and
women with men.

MICHAEL
[*Overlapping*]
Are you coming to the point?

BERNARD
[*Calmly*]
Michael, let Jason say what he wants to say.

EMORY
Yeah.

JASON
[*Pressing on*]
For Larry, the fight for legalized gay marriage was about protection:
tax exemptions, benefits, inheritances...

MICHAEL
Now, wait just a minute!

DONALD
Michael!

JASON
[*Accelerating, overlapping*]
Basically being fed up with gays getting screwed out of what any
spouse who had a piece of paper would be entitled to!

MICHAEL
[*Interrupting*]
Listen, *poster boy*, this is not a pep rally, nor a protest! You are *not*
on a platform *nor* a soapbox, you are in *my* living room, and I will
not have you haranguing or handcuffing yourself to the
Biedermeier!
[*HANK stands.*]

HANK
[*With authority*]
That's really enough out of the two of you!
[*The room immediately quiets.*]

[*Coolly*]
Jason, you're right about Larry, but you *are* a bit off track. And
Michael, as usual, you're just *out of line.*

MICHAEL
[*Thinks, sighs*]
Of course I am. I apologize.

JASON
So do I.

HAROLD
[*After a moment*]
Thanks, Hank. I was hoping someone would kick them *both* in the
nuts!

MICHAEL
[*Sarcastically*]
What do you want to be when *you* grow up, Harold?

HAROLD
[*To MICHAEL, deadly*]
Broad-minded.

HANK
[*After a moment*]
Yes. Broad-minded. Larry greatly appreciated the "differentness" of being gay. So he didn't want to ape heterosexual conventions—particularly marital ones. Larry knew that a real bond between us had nothing to do with a piece of paper—that it was only important that he and I be married in our minds. He knew being wed had nothing to do with legality—only to do with the personal, private, unique contract between two consenting grown-ups. And the ground rules you make yourself. And they can't be the same for all. Maybe it's only now that I can say something to him...to *myself*. That through it all—faithfulness, fear, infidelity, forgiveness—our *marriage* was never threatened. We were together a long time on our own terms.

JASON
Hear, hear!

MICHAEL
[*To JASON*]
Will you shut the fuck up?!

DONALD
Michael, please!

MICHAEL
Oh, all right! Cut my throat. See if *I* care.

EMORY
Let's all raise our glasses in a final toast.
[*Everyone stands, raises his glass, no matter what it contains, wine or water or Belgian lemon soda...*]

EMORY
[*Rises*]
To Larry. Peaceful at last.
[*Everyone drinks. HANK goes over to JASON and puts his arms around him to hug him for a long moment. RICK watches closely.*]

EMORY
[*Waving his camera*]
Photo op! Photo op!

HAROLD
[*Covers his face with EMORY's fan*]
No pictures, *please*!

208

MICHAEL
    [*With disgust*]
Snapshots?! Ugh!!

EMORY
Hush! Both of you!
    [*Corralling the group*]
Now, don't everybody break up! Move in! Move in!

BERNARD
Come on, Michael! Come on, you guys! Bunch up!

DONALD
Orgy time!

HAROLD
    [*To JASON*]
If only.
    [*The group starts to assemble opposite the stairs.*]

RICK
    [*To EMORY*]
You're the one that ought to be in the picture!

EMORY
Don't worry!
    [*He snaps a timing button, sets the camera on an eye-level rung of
    the stairs and rushes toward the center of the group. He lunges into
    a rope of interwoven arms and is bounced back to his feet, like a
    dazed, bejeweled prizefighter. He grabs RICK and JASON around
    their necks and holds on as the group lets out a raucous
    "Whooaahhh!"*]

HAROLD
    [*Quickly*]
Might know you'd take center stage!

EMORY
    [*Quickly*]
Shut up and lick your lips!

BERNARD
Hold it, everybody!

EMORY
And say, "Lesbian!"

THE ENTIRE GROUP
[*In unison, producing frozen smiles*]
LESBIAN!!
[*The flash goes off! A cheer goes up!* EMORY *rushes back to the camera, the group disperses.* RICK *slides open the terrace doors, goes outside.*]

BERNARD
[*To* MICHAEL]
What happened to Scott?

MICHAEL
[*Coolly*]
He had to go. He asked me to say his goodbyes.

HAROLD
I never even got a chance to say *hello!*

EMORY
And I'm sure you're heartbroken.

HAROLD
[*Feigning naïveté*]
Why, whatever do you mean?
[RICK *enters from the terrace with the bottle of champagne.*]

JASON
Yeah, what *do* you mean, Harold?

EMORY
Hallie doesn't care for the boy.

HAROLD
Scott is an acquired taste—which I have somehow failed to acquire.
[*Bluntly, to* EMORY]
No, I don't. And you don't either.

EMORY
And neither does Bernard.

BERNARD
I've never said a word against Scott!

EMORY
[*To* BERNARD]
But you don't like him. I can tell. Larry liked him, I guess.

HAROLD
Larry just liked to *look* at him.

HANK
[*Correcting simply*]
No, Larry *liked* him. He thought someone would be good for
Michael.
[*A pause.* RICK *pours himself a flute of champagne, listens with
interest.*]

JASON
Scott's really kind of crazy. I mean, like, nuts. Really.

EMORY
Well, who isn't a little?
[*Gestures with one hand*]
I'm schizophrenic.
[*Gestures with the other*]
And so am *I*!

JASON
[*Continuing*]
I found that out when I sold him my bike.
[MICHAEL *eyes* JASON *suspiciously.*]

HAROLD
[*Bluntly, to* JASON, *for* MICHAEL's *benefit*]
Scott's a crawler. And an opportunist.

MICHAEL
Don't hold back, Harold.

JASON
It's the crystal that makes him crazy.

MICHAEL
[*Seething*]
How would you know that?!

JASON
When he came to our apartment to pick up the bike, his eyelids
were on the ceiling. He sat on the floor for four hours playing a
video game and didn't blink once. My boyfriend knows his dealer.

BERNARD
I thought he was clean.

JASON
That's *his* story.

MICHAEL
[*Snaps*]
Scott does not lie!

JASON
[*To MICHAEL, flatly*]
Scott's the kind of guy who steals your drugs and then helps you
look for them!
[*DONALD freshens his drink with gin.*]

DONALD
[*To MICHAEL*]
You don't know when he's lying and when he isn't.

RICK
He must tell the truth sometime.

HAROLD
Only when his imagination flags.

MICHAEL
[*To all, seriously facetious*]
Scott is just a welcome antidote to heartiness.
[*RICK takes his guitar case upstairs.*]

DONALD
He uses you, Michael. He plays you like a violin.

EMORY
He couldn't. Michael had all his old violins made into shoe trees.

HAROLD
Scott has made *Michael* into a shoe tree. It's one thing to get fucked.
It's another to get fucked *over.*

MICHAEL
[*For DONALD's benefit*]
None of us ever likes any of our so-called "other" friends.

HANK
I like everybody and everybody's friends. Everybody here, I mean.
My friends and their friends.

MICHAEL
That's because you're not a cunt, Hank.

DONALD
We all get rattled when we show up with a new trick, or a twinkie.

MICHAEL
Scott is neither a trick nor a twinkie, thank you very much!

EMORY
I guess you struck a nerve, Donald.

HAROLD
I think it was Jason who did the root canal.

RICK
        [*Coming downstairs*]
Is that how you think of us? That we're nothing but cheap tricks?

JASON
        [*To RICK*]
Speak for yourself.

RICK
I am speaking for myself.
        [*To group*]
But, God, how could anybody's younger friends stand up next to you guys?

JASON
        [*Drolly*]
You mean for honesty and loyalty and charity?

RICK
I mean for *longevity*.

EMORY
Longevity?! You're not talking about old fucking redwoods again, are you?!

RICK
Longevity of friendship.

EMORY
I'll have you know I'm still in my deep forties.

BERNARD
If you're fortysomething, this must be your second time on earth!

DONALD
[*To* RICK]
It's been a longer run for some of us than for others.

BERNARD
We do resent our "other friends." For once, you're absolutely right,
Michael. We're proprietary as hell about each other. We're a closed
corporation. We don't like anybody else. How could we, when we
can barely stand each other?

EMORY
Don't be sil, we adore each other.

JASON
[*Sardonically*]
Oh, yeah, sure you do!

BERNARD
We do! We just don't like outsiders. And not just you.
[*To* EMORY]
How do you *really* feel about my wife?

EMORY
I adore your wife! How can you ask such a question? Women are
not threats to gay men. "Other women." I don't know why. It's
strange, but any guy I was ever interested in could have had all the
girlfriends he wanted—just not boyfriends. We just get nervous to a
degree when one of us shows up with a twinkie.
[*Sees* MICHAEL *glaring*]
Eh...a recruit.

BERNARD
You wouldn't know what a real recruit was if you fell over one. I
doubt if you know what the words "military service" mean.

EMORY
For your information, I've fallen over my share of recruits and serv-
iced the military quite patriotically! Oh, Mary, don't ask and *don't
tell*!

JASON
Do you have a patent on camp?

EMORY
[*To* JASON, *cuttingly*]
Yeah, it's in *black* patent, sweetie! Some of us were more outrageous before Stonewall! Some of us were just as in-your-face as *you* ever hoped to be!

JASON
Flaming with resentment?

EMORY
[*With an edge*]
We were funny, dear.
[*Looks over the group; pointedly*]
Now there're not so many of us left.

JASON
[*Re* EMORY's *kind*]
Mmm, you're an endangered species!

EMORY
[*Tough*]
Listen, kiddo, before there were marches, there was a band.

JASON
[*To* EMORY]
And you were in the front line, were you? Well, congratulations.

EMORY
You don't have to get all Dorothy Darling with me now. I just happened to be walking by, minding my own business. Wearing a dress, of course, but minding my own business.

MICHAEL
Just out for the evening, trawling for love.

EMORY
We weren't just lifestyles *that* night, we were *news*!

MICHAEL
[*Aside, to* JASON]
Stay off those floats! It's bad PR!
[*Considering* JASON]
A parade with three hundred thousand people in attendance, and the TV news has to focus on ten people in leather and chains and three of the ugliest drags known to man!

EMORY

Well, Stonewall changed my life. In fact, it brought me *to* life. It brought my hidden talents into a follow spot. I used to have to pay to get out of jail for doing what I *get paid* to do now!

RICK

I admire what you did. It took guts.

JASON

You may not be into leather or drag, Michael. You may not approve. But, like it or not, it's part of the real world.

DONALD

The public wants *theater*! Not dentists in their double-knit suits.

JASON

Yeah, if you want the boy next door, go next door.

EMORY

Didn't Joan Crawford say that?

MICHAEL

No, she said, "Just who is kidding *whom*."
        [*Some mild laughter. Suddenly,* RICK *speaks…*]

RICK

I lie too. About who I am and what I am.

MICHAEL

What are you talking about?

RICK

Well…I'm not Vietnamese-American. My father wasn't an officer in the military. My mother didn't speak French. I just took a course at the Alliance. I'm Filipino.

HAROLD

So?

RICK

        [*Calmly*]
So I've lied about who I am all my adult life.

HANK

Why?

RICK

I always wanted to be *beyond* Polynesian, I wanted to be more "high born." More aristocratic. Do you know what the second largest population in Hong Kong is—after Americans? Filipino workers. Filipino *domestic* workers.

BERNARD

When it comes to domestic workers, what do you think about *my* people?

EMORY

You've never denied your background, Bernard.

BERNARD

I guess we all wonder just how honest we've been with ourselves. How much we've denied. I wish I could be more like Larry in that department. More up-front, no matter what.
    [*Reflectively*]
When I was a kid in Grosse Pointe, there used to be a Chinese couple—who worked for the same family my mother did, the Dahlbecks. And their oldest kid, the son, used to refer to them behind their backs as "the Slits." And when he did, I used to laugh. God only knows what he said behind *my* back about *me*.
    [*Laughs bitterly at thought*]
I wonder if he used to laugh that way about the little colored hypocrite who had a crush on him?
    [*After a moment*]
I went home last Christmas to see my mother. While I was there, I stopped by to say hello to him. He sold the big house and now lives alone in a big condo but still has two servants who live in.

JASON

Two servants! How can two people have a full-time job, working for just one guy? What's there to do?

BERNARD

Dust. Answer the phone. Take the abuse.

RICK
    [*Sardonically*]
Oh, well, *that's* always a full-time job.

BERNARD

Yeah, in some people's lives that's a *career*! Peter's a bitter and difficult old man now.

HANK
You think he's gay?

BERNARD
No, not at all.

EMORY
He couldn't be. Bernard described his furniture.

RICK
[*Reflectively*]
There's even discrimination within the gay community; a bouncer
just assumed my cock wasn't big enough to get into a leather bar. So
he didn't let me in. God only knows what *he* was.

HAROLD
A bastard, for sure.

RICK
I've thought about plastic surgery—you know, "Westernize" my
eyes.

HAROLD
I'd trade places with you just as you are. Oh, to have your skin. Oh,
just to be your age—with your skin! I understand the contempt this
country feels for the old. Getting old is the greatest sin in America.
Worse than dying poor.
[*Looks at JASON*]
And why not, as long as Calvin Klein continues to make us feel
awful about ourselves? But since we're no longer in hiding and it
appears that we're going to live, what are we going to *do* with ourselves?

EMORY
It's not easy when you're asked to leave the dance floor. Why was it
that with Larry, his age didn't seem to matter?

HAROLD
It did sometimes. And when it did, it hurt. It just didn't matter to
everyone.
[*Smiles at HANK; to EMORY*]
Larry was handsome, and you are not. Nor is Michael. Nor am I.

MICHAEL
Harold, you have an *obsession* with beauty. You always have.

JASON
   [*Tauntingly*]
You got something against beauty, Michael?

HAROLD
   [*Coolly*]
Thanks, Jason, but I can bridge this gap for myself. One, Michael,
I'm an American. And, two, I'm human. And, three, I don't lie
about such things. People don't want anything ugly. Clothes or cars
or whatever. Of course, they may choose something that's fucking
hideous or tacky or tasteless to others, but to them, you can bet it's
beautiful. It's sexy! It sings! It *sells*!
   [*Reflectively*]
The beauties of the world can never know us. And we can never
know them. Because they never, ever have to deal with the nature
of our agony in coming to grips with our baggage. Every day we are
banking the fires. They live a life sustained in an oblivious, effort-
less, cozy glow—being worshiped, and adored, and catered to.
Being...*wanted*.

RICK
   [*"In-the-know" non sequitur*]
Older gay men want younger men—just like older straight men
want younger women.

BERNARD
And older women want good-looking young guys.

HAROLD
Well, love is one thing. Getting your pulse jump-started is another.

RICK
Yeah.

HAROLD
   [*After a moment*]
My outside has never reflected what's inside my brain, my aesthetic
sense of myself. When I look in the mirror I do not see what I see
in my mind's eye. I have never liked anything that fails to please
me visually—including my own looks. I don't want to *have* Brad
Pitt—I want to *look like* Brad Pitt. Anybody who says exteriors don't
matter is full of shit. And you can quote me. Fulsomely.

JASON
   [*Looking outside*]
The rain has stopped.

EMORY
[*Generally*]
En voiture!
[*Everyone starts to shift, stretch, make noise…*]

HANK
Could I say one quick thing before we break up?

BERNARD
Hang on, everyone!
[*The room quiets…*]

HANK
We'll go out of here, and all of this will be forgotten. But no matter, this was *done* for him. And for us. What we take away from here— the difference in the way we feel…and aren't even yet aware of— that's what this was about. Thank you all for being here. And thank you for not having asked all the wrong questions.
[*A final round of applause as* JASON *slides open the terrace doors*]

RICK
[*Re weather*]
It's gonna be a nice day after all!
[*Everyone begins to break up and move.*]

[HAROLD *goes to* JASON, *says a silent goodbye.* RICK *shakes hands with* HANK…]

BERNARD
[*To* EMORY]
You're not walking out of here with me looking like the eleventh-best-dressed woman!

EMORY
This is *not* my daytime look.

BERNARD
Well, get on your daytime *traveling* look and hurry up about it!

EMORY
I won't be a minute! Don't get in a tiz! I've just gotta tissue off my base and find my petit point.
[EMORY *turns for the stairs.* HAROLD *and* JASON *finish their silent goodbye,* JASON *reaches for his cigarettes, takes out one, lights up, and goes outside.* MICHAEL *furiously fans the smoke in his wake.* HAROLD *stops* EMORY *at the base of the stairs…*]

HAROLD
    [*To* MICHAEL]
I hate to dine and dash, but I've got to get back to my blond house-
guest.

MICHAEL
    [*Still fanning smoke*]
Why rush?! You might be on *time*!

EMORY
Now, now, you two. We've already had dinner and a show.

HAROLD
    [*To* EMORY]
Gimme a kiss, puppy.

EMORY
    [*Kisses* HAROLD *on cheek, hurries up the stairs*]
I wanna hear how it works out. All the lurid details.

HAROLD
    [*To* EMORY]
I'll call you and give you a blow-by-blow account—oh, catch me,
Dr. Freud, I'm slipping!
    [HAROLD *hugs* HANK, *turns away. He picks up his rain cape and
    umbrella.* EMORY *runs upstairs and peels off his eyelashes as he
    enters the bathroom.*]

BERNARD
Bye, Hallie.

HAROLD
    [*To* BERNARD]
Bye, love. Now, I don't want you cheating on your wife while she's
out of town on an errand of mercy.
    [*Dryly*]
Donald. We've got to stop meeting like this.

DONALD
Yeah, Harold, ain't it the truth.

HAROLD
You think I'm kidding!
    [DONALD *shakes his head, moves away.* JASON *turns to* BERNARD.]

JASON
[*To* BERNARD]
Will you help me bring in the bar cart?

BERNARD
Yeah, and it won't even send me into the well-known "downward
spiral."
[BERNARD *follows* JASON; *they exit to the terrace.*]

RICK
Nice to see you, Harold.

HAROLD
Sayonara, Ricky. Sorry I can't say it in Tagalog. We should visit your
homeland together—I'm mad to do the Pacific Rim. If you're ever
in the Village, I'm in the book.

RICK
Don't be surprised if you hear from me.

HAROLD
Young man, nothing surprises *me*.

RICK
Michael, what'd you do with the rest of the raincoats?

MICHAEL
Hung 'em on the shower door.
[RICK *goes upstairs.*]

HAROLD
[*To* MICHAEL]
Let's talk sometime within the next eighteen-hour window.

MICHAEL
Get out of here!
[*They air-kiss on both cheeks.*]

HAROLD
Constant touch. Missing you already!
[HAROLD *whips on his cape with a great flourish and is out the
door.* JASON *and* BERNARD *lift the bar cart over the terrace door
jamb.* HANK *puts on his coat.* RICK *lingers at the top of the stairs,
looking down at* HANK.]

BERNARD
[*To* HANK]
How are you getting home?

HANK
Subway, I guess.

BERNARD
We'll share a cab and drop you off.

HANK
Thanks, but I'm way out of your way. Besides, I really want to be
by myself.
      [*BERNARD nods.*]

DONALD
So long, Hank...

HANK
Donald.
      [*They hug.* DONALD *turns back to the bar cart, takes the silver casse-
      role chafing dish off the cart and into the kitchen.*]

BERNARD
[*Loudly toward upstairs*]
Let's *GO*, Emory! Thanks, Michael. I apologize if I lost it there for
a moment.

MICHAEL
Amends are not necessary, Bernard. You know I appreciate your
concern. By the way, are *you* still in therapy?

BERNARD
Just low-maintenance. Ciao, baby! Don't say it *ain't* been!
      [*They kiss on the cheek.* BERNARD *turns to* HANK, *and they silently
      and fondly hug each other.* EMORY *comes out of the bathroom, heads
      downstairs carrying his small makeup case, his face clean.* RICK
      enters the bathroom, closes the door.]

EMORY
[*To* MICHAEL]
Listen, *cheri*, it's been seamless. Absolutely seamless. When I go, I'd
like to have a celebration exactly like this one.

223

MICHAEL
We have next Thursday open.

EMORY
Oh, that hurt worse than a slap with a suede glove!
    [*EMORY crosses to kiss* HANK *on the cheek.*]

EMORY
    [*Blows* MICHAEL *a kiss*]
Bye, dear. Stay pretty.
    [*BERNARD shakes his head, as he and* EMORY *are out the front door.*]

HANK
Some assortment, this group!

MICHAEL
Like a cheap box of chocolates. Some dark, some white. Even an exotic honey-dipped confection.

HANK
    [*Reflectively*]
Some soft, some brittle.

MICHAEL
    [*Pleasantly*]
And all either too sweet or too *bitter*sweet. And that includes this old bonbon.

HANK
But we change whether we like it or not.

MICHAEL
You mean we get *older* whether we like it or not.

HANK
No, I mean we change. Change *is* possible. Growth *is* possible. I believe that, Michael.

MICHAEL
Some people change. Some people never change. Some just sit on the fence. I don't think we ever quite shake off whatever it is we settle on being somewhere around the age of three. It's all over by then. *I* believe that.

HANK
[*Salutes* MICHAEL *with his stem glass*]
Theorize, and drink champagne.
[HANK *drains his glass.*]

MICHAEL
Listen, you don't think I've had *too much* analysis, do you? Or gone
a step too far? Like, *thirteen*. You know how I always overdo everything.

HANK
Well, none of it did you any harm. It couldn't have. It was either
that or die.

MICHAEL
Hank, I've never told you how much I admire the way you dealt
with Larry's extracurricular activities.

HANK
It may have been a marriage of now and then untrue bodies, but it
was one of constantly true minds. Messy. Like life.
[*Changes subject*]
Listen, there isn't any possible way to say…

MICHAEL
[*Cuts him off, quietly*]
No. Don't. Please.

HANK
I'm not. Not *now*. I'm going to try to write my feelings down and
send them to you—and I know that's risky with a writer, but it's
what I want to do.

MICHAEL
Oh, Hank…have no fear. I want to thank *you*. I won't forget this
afternoon. For so many reasons.
[MICHAEL *and* HANK *embrace and part.* MICHAEL *opens the door for*
HANK, *who goes out.* MICHAEL *closes the door as* JASON *enters from
the terrace.*]

JASON
Everybody gone?

MICHAEL
Well, the tide's not *completely* out.

JASON

Why do you dislike me so? I don't think it's my politics. I actually think we're on the same side.

MICHAEL

The only thing we share is our anger.

JASON

You know, you might be useful if you were going in the right direction.

MICHAEL

Don't patronize me.

JASON

Hardly. Your contentment, your complacency may have allowed you to survive, but they won't get me through. I've got to do something about the way things are.

MICHAEL

You dismiss us—me and my kind—and worse yet, you make us responsible for everything you take for granted! How do you think you got it?

JASON

Well, you and your cronies have sadly outlived your purpose.

MICHAEL

So you'd be just as glad if we didn't exist. We're in your way.

JASON

That's right. You're expendable.

MICHAEL

Listen, Jason, if it weren't for boys like us, there wouldn't be men like you.

JASON

Now who's being patronizing?

MICHAEL
[*Bluntly*]
You're the one who stole Scott's bike, aren't you?

JASON

What?

MICHAEL

You did drugs with him, and he passed out, and you took his bike, probably thinking it was still yours.

JASON

Michael, I don't do drugs, and I'm not a thief. I take an oath on my life—on my lover's life!

MICHAEL

If I didn't like you before, now I really have no use for you.

JASON

Well, if you won't listen to reason—
        [*JASON starts to leave.*]

MICHAEL
        [*Softer tone*]
Wait! I *will* listen to reason.

JASON
        [*Stops and turns*]
I sold him my old bike, which, I assume, was paid for with your money. He came by to look at it, said he'd think it over, and left. Half an hour later he called and said he'd take it. When I took it by his place, he asked if I'd like to do some "K" with him and go dancing, but I said no. I left the bike with him and left him alone. I'm not lying.
        [*DONALD enters from the kitchen.*]

DONALD
        [*To JASON*]
Are you staying in the city or going back to the Hamptons?

JASON
I'm going back.
        [*Puts on raincoat*]
But I have to stop and pick up the mail and get a sweater. It's colder on the island than I thought. Why—you want to get the Jitney together? Or take a train?

DONALD
I drove into town. My car's in a garage between First and Second. I don't mind waiting, if you don't mind driving. I've had a little more to drink than I thought.

JASON
I don't mind at all!

DONALD
You ought to come over to my place. I have a fire almost every
evening. And I have lots of sweaters you're welcome to. Not as
many as Michael, of course.

JASON
I wouldn't want to go in Michael's sweater closet for fear of being
killed by falling Missonis.
        [DONALD *laughs a little drunkenly.* MICHAEL *is slightly disturbed by*
        DONALD's *condition.*]

DONALD
        [*To* MICHAEL, *drolly*]
I washed the stemware by hand.

MICHAEL
You don't still do windows, do you?

DONALD
Thanks...for the memories.

MICHAEL
Say no more.

DONALD
Where's *my* coat?
        [DONALD *stumbles on a rung of the stairs.*]

MICHAEL
        [*Sotto voce to* JASON, *caringly*]
Will you...uh...will you be sure that he...

JASON
        [*Nods; sotto voce*]
Yeah, yeah, sure.

DONALD
        [*Turns to them with dignity*]
Surely, I'm not the first person you've ever seen fall *up* the stairs.

MICHAEL
Donald, I don't think you *had* a coat. Take one of mine if you like.
    [*Dryly*]
And there's no danger of avalanche. You don't have to hazard the
Missoni section for the rain gear.

DONALD
I had a blazer. I know I could find it if it had hair around it.

JASON
    [*Picks up DONALD's blazer*]
Here it is.
        [*DONALD crosses to JASON, who helps him on with his jacket.*]

DONALD
Thank you, dear boy.

JASON
So you're in real estate?
    [*DONALD nods*]
You think a good bar and deli would go out there?

DONALD
    [*Friendly*]
We'll do some pub crawling and see what's on its last legs. I know
them all. I've long considered writing a book: *The Alcoholic's Guide to
the Hamptons*. Not only furnish a complete listing of the best bars,
but also have a vital statistics page with all the bar *obits*, that is, *cele-
brations* of bars that've died during the year.

JASON
Sounds great. I've been a flight attendant, a host in a restaurant,
and, of course, a bartender. I think I could make a go of it with a
place of my own. I'm good with the public.

DONALD
I can see why—you have charm. Not an easy thing to come by.

JASON
    [*Smiles*]
It's still raining pretty hard. Why don't you give me the ticket for
your car and wait here. I'll be right back for you.

DONALD
[*Hands over ticket*]
With the greatest of pleasure. No need to come up, just buzz and
I'll go down.

JASON
And maybe have a cup of coffee in the meantime.
[*For MICHAEL's benefit*]
There's plenty left in that nice, simple pot.
[*DONALD laughs at MICHAEL's annoyance. JASON goes out the front
door.*]

MICHAEL
[*To DONALD*]
Well, that's the last you'll see of him or that vulgar Lincoln
Continental.

DONALD
[*Crosses to MICHAEL*]
Tell me the truth, Michael. You miss it, don't you?

MICHAEL
On occasion, yes. On a nice occasion—like today or a birthday or
New Year's—something clear and chilled to perfection doesn't seem
half bad. Yes, Donald, I miss that fine, cozy, boozy feeling when it
was at its best. But it's not possible. I'm a drunk, and I can't drink.
Ever, ever again.

DONALD
Pity.
[*Smiles*]
It was a very nice afternoon, Michael. And we got through it without ever using the word "dysfunctional." It was just what Larry
would have liked. Done just the way he would have liked it, with
just the people he liked.

MICHAEL
[*Tongue-in-cheek, re his expensive wristwatch*]
You know, I like my Cartier watch better than any of those people I
invited this afternoon. And I *don't* have a Rolex, no matter what
your new boyfriend says.

DONALD
Didn't you hear Jason? He already has a lover.

MICHAEL
    [*Looks at his Cartier*]
Yeah, they ought to be halfway to Key West by now.

DONALD
    [*Lightly*]
Michael, I trust him.
    [*Laughs feebly*]
Once upon a time I'd have had a chance with someone like Jason.
But these days, I hardly stack up to Larry. But…I must have some-
thing he's interested in.

MICHAEL
I don't think it's your mind—*or* your body.

DONALD
Well, if he thinks I'm rich, he's in for an epiphany. I'm just cozy.
And I can be helpful to him. And who knows, maybe he does *like*
older guys. He liked Larry.
    [*With meaning*]
Some other young men did too.

MICHAEL
    [*Oblivious*]
I guess I was just always so goddamned jealous of Larry. Of his
looks. Of his body. How he seemed to be blessed. How even his
toes were beautiful. Of how he seemed to get every guy he ever
wanted. Of how he and Hank seem to beat the odds and stay
together.

DONALD
You know, if you read Christopher Isherwood's diaries, you really
wake up to find out nothing for nobody is ever easy in life.

MICHAEL
You know, Donald, you're not the only one who can recite the
alphabet! Isherwood and his lover, Don Bachardy, were always my
ideal couple. But I was stunned to learn their relationship wasn't
what I thought it was. Not what I thought I'd *missed*. You must
think it absurd that I was shocked to find out…

DONALD
To find out that they were human too?

MICHAEL
Yeah, I guess so.

DONALD

Nobody has it all, Michael. Each of us has a lot to survive. Nobody escapes.

MICHAEL

Yeah. Not even beautiful Larry. It's a shame to never have made a success of love with someone. But it just doesn't work for me. It can work for others. In fact, for others, it's essential. But it just can't work for me. It never has. For me, it's always been better to travel hopefully than to ever arrive.
[*The downstairs door buzzes.*]

DONALD
[*Facetiously*]

That would be my car and driver. Or should I say, my *designated* driver.

MICHAEL

You worry me, Donald. Be careful.

DONALD

You've mellowed, Michael. And that's to your credit. But don't ever lose your anger. Without that, you're a living dead man. Not a vampire. Something worse.

MICHAEL

I know. I know. Now, listen, keep your hands to yourself on the L.I.E. I don't want you dead in a car crash—even when you're not driving.

DONALD

Yessir.
[*Lightly*]
To be continued.
[*They hug, and Donald exits silently. Michael closes the door as Rick comes out of the bathroom and down the stairs.*]

RICK

I hope you don't mind, I opened one of those little bars of soap, Michael. Like, I couldn't resist the label.

MICHAEL

That's what they're there for.

RICK

Thanks. Nice hand towels too. French?

MICHAEL

Italian. Thank *you* for the song. Maybe you ought to consider a really sensible career move, like show business.

RICK

I've got other ideas—all thanks to Larry.

MICHAEL

Good on you, as the Australians say.
[*RICK goes to the door, turns to* MICHAEL.]

RICK

By the way, I couldn't help overhearing...Jason was telling you the truth. He didn't take Scott's bike—*I* did.

MICHAEL

You?

RICK

It was my first time to do crystal, and I never want to do it again. Honestly. That's definitely not my scene. But I just couldn't resist the temptation, the curiosity. So we went to his place.

MICHAEL

Why did you take his bike?

RICK

I can't explain it. It was crazy. I was speeding—and in a hurry on top of it. Scott was in the shower, and the bike was by the door, and I just took it. But I took it *back*! I didn't *want* it! I didn't even remember where he lived. I had to ask Larry.

MICHAEL

Did you have sex with Scott too?

RICK

I wasn't interested.

MICHAEL

You knew Scott before today? You met him at the hospital at night?
[*RICK nods.*]

MICHAEL
[*Shocked*]

He never told me he went there without me.

RICK

Maybe like Larry, he kept his friends compartmentalized too.

MICHAEL

I guess he *did*.

RICK

At first, I thought that he was Larry's lover, but then I began to see Hank and found out the story.

MICHAEL

Funny, I'd never even considered it—Scott and Larry.

RICK

I don't really know if they'd ever had a thing or not. I doubt it. Scott never said so.

MICHAEL

The two of you talked about it?

RICK
    [*Nods*]

The night we did drugs. The night I "borrowed" his bike.

MICHAEL
    [*Incredulous*]

But you didn't even say hello to each other today.

RICK

I said "Hi" to him outside. He didn't want you to know we knew each other—or why.

MICHAEL

Scott still isn't aware you're the one?

RICK
    [*Shakes his head*]

I never had a chance to explain.

MICHAEL

You don't think Larry and Scott had a thing, do you?

RICK
    [*Shakes his head*]

I just think Larry was a soft touch.

MICHAEL
Scott asked him for money?

RICK
He just told him what a hard time he was having making it through school, and Larry felt sorry for him. Frankly, I think Scott just wanted it to buy drugs.
    [*Suddenly, the door buzzes.* MICHAEL *goes to the wall panel, pushes the door release button.*]

MICHAEL
Goodbye, Rick.

RICK
I hope we see each other again sometime.

MICHAEL
Yes...yes, of course.
    [RICK *pulls on his coat. The apartment bell rings.*]

MICHAEL
Now what?!
    [MICHAEL *opens the door.*]

    [*Surprised*]
Hank! What's wrong?

HANK
Nothing. The flowers—

MICHAEL
Oh, I can bring them over in the morning—you don't have to bother with them now.

HANK
No, no, you keep them. I just want Patsy and Jessica's note. It was very beautiful. They must have put a lot of thought into it. I guess I'd forget my head if it wasn't...
    [RICK *picks up the envelope, hands it to* HANK.]

HANK
Thanks, Rick.

RICK
I'll walk you to the subway. I go your way.

HANK
Okay. Good night, Michael.

RICK
Yes, and thanks again.

MICHAEL
You're welcome, Rick. And *bon chance*.
>[*HANK smiles at RICK, puts his hand on RICK's shoulder, and they go
>out. MICHAEL turns to survey the damage (which isn't all that bad),
>and exits the terrace doors. For a moment, the stage is empty, then the
>doorbell rings. MICHAEL enters from the terrace with a stack of plates
>and takes them into the kitchen. The bell rings again. MICHAEL enters,
>turns the lights down low, crosses to the door to open it.*]

MICHAEL
[*Crestfallen*]
Ohh, *you* again! How'd you get in this time?!

HAROLD
Hank and Rick were just leaving together. Interesting.

MICHAEL
[*Deliberately*]
The...party...is...over.
>[*HAROLD "casually" enters. MICHAEL steps into the corridor, looks about.*]

HAROLD
Now it's so dark in here, you need night-vision glasses. I take it you
were expecting someone other than myself just now.
>[*MICHAEL comes back into the room, closes the door, flips on the
>lights, turns to HAROLD...*]

MICHAEL
[*Ignores the remark*]
I thought I'd gotten rid of you.

HAROLD
[*Puts on dark glasses*]
I guess so. When you opened the door, your face sank like a lost cause.

MICHAEL
[*Matter-of-fact*]
I thought it might be Scott.

HAROLD
Don't fret, he'll be back. He's not through with you yet.
[*MICHAEL is annoyed, tries not to show it.*]

MICHAEL
[*Reasonably*]
I love him, Harold.

HAROLD
But he doesn't love you. He never has, and he never will, no matter
how much you invest in him. And that's the plain and simple truth.
If you want someone, go after someone you can get.

MICHAEL
I don't *want* anyone I can get!

HAROLD
[*Offhandedly*]
Who'd Jason leave with?

MICHAEL
Donald.

HAROLD
Not so interesting. But interesting.

MICHAEL
God, Jason's so common, I bet he smokes in the shower.

HAROLD
Listen, every time I look in Scott's face I think of Easter Island.

MICHAEL
[*Testily*]
When I met Scott, I knew instantly he had intelligence and potential.

HAROLD
Well, he *had* seen a movie with subtitles.

MICHAEL
I thought you were so eager to get home to that blond who was with
you at the service!

HAROLD
I am. He's almost *obscenely* sexy, dontcha think?

MICHAEL
[*Magnanimously*]
I'm not being judgmental about your choice of companions, Harold.
You know I don't give a good goddamn about morals, but *taste* is
everything!
[*HAROLD sucks a tooth*]
What're you going to do with that boy? Tonight, I mean. When you
finally get home.

HAROLD
We *may* pull a condom over the entire apartment and have safe sex,
or I *may* just take my 800-milligram Xanax with a tall beverage and
isolate.

MICHAEL
Well, I hope you're careful. After all, who knows about his status?

HAROLD
I know his status, and he knows mine. But maybe I'll just have to
settle for chinning myself on his nipple rings.

MICHAEL
And you gave that trash the key to your apartment?

HAROLD
Scott has the key to yours, doesn't he?

MICHAEL
You can spare me any character analysis of Scott.

HAROLD
That oughta be like a dial tone.

MICHAEL
You disapprove, like Donald.

HAROLD
I don't do *anything* like Donald! It would be too easy to call Scott a
cock-teaser. It would also be unfair, because I think he has *some*
consideration for you in his own mixed-up, sorry way.

MICHAEL
You just think I'm a fool.

HAROLD
All you need are bells and a scepter.

238

MICHAEL
[*Tongue-in-cheek bravura*]
I like a *challenge*!
[*Grimly*]
He let me down about school. Again.

HAROLD
He'll let you down again and again and again. And you'll forgive
him again and again and again. I think that's what love is all about.

MICHAEL
You've never let me down, Harold.

HAROLD
You never tried to put me through college.

MICHAEL
[*Short*]
What did you come back for?! Are you still *stoned*!?

HAROLD
I wish I were, but I didn't want to blur the edges before I returned.
I wanted to be completely...well, as you always put it—I wanted
my faculties functioning at their maximum natural capacity.
[*There is a more awkward pause, a silence, between them as
HAROLD looks directly at MICHAEL.*]

HAROLD
[*After a moment*]
I've got AIDS. It's still with us, you know—despite the dancing in
the streets.
[*Reacts to MICHAEL's expression*]
Now, don't go and get all...

MICHAEL
[*Interrupting sharply*]
I'm not going to go and get all anything!
[*Contrary to what he says, MICHAEL seems dazed.*]

HAROLD
Well, for God's sake, don't cry.

MICHAEL
You know I never cry in a *real* crisis.

HAROLD
[*Indirectly*]
It's the lies we tell ourselves that really matter.

MICHAEL
[*Ignores this*]
What about all the new medications?

HAROLD
It's probably a tad too late for the cocktail hour. Besides, who knows if I'm one of those who can tolerate the mix.

MICHAEL
[*Stupefied*]
How long have you known?

HAROLD
Two months.

MICHAEL
Two months!

HAROLD
Yeah, I'm a tricky little thing.

MICHAEL
How do you feel? Do you *know* how you feel?

HAROLD
[*Removes dark glasses*]
In an odd way, like Hank said, I feel relieved. I've spent a lifetime thinking about death. One thing I know I'm going to try to do: be a better Jew. And by that I don't mean run to temple every time I have an anxiety attack. What I mean is—try to practice some of the things I really believe in.

MICHAEL
Are you gonna get religion now so you can go to heaven?

HAROLD
Not at all. Catholics are worried about what comes after—you know, carry your cross today, and go to the party later. Jews are more focused on the here and now—business, family, food. All that kosher stuff is based on living well. I'm going to try to live well in the here and now and let tomorrow take care of itself.

MICHAEL
I'm all for that. You mean you knew when you went to St. Bart's?!

HAROLD
I didn't go to St. Bart's in the West Indies. I went to St. Vincent's in the West Village. Well, the paramedics had to haul me away. I had Pneumocystis. I had to stay for the full twenty-one days.. Then home for another...

MICHAEL
Why in the world didn't you tell me?! Why didn't you call me?

HAROLD
I did call you.

MICHAEL
From the *hospital*?! I thought you were calling from...

HAROLD
That's what I *wanted* you to think. I certainly didn't want to see anybody, and I didn't want anybody to see me. I was too sick. But tonight, well, I wanted you to know.

MICHAEL
[*Blankly*]
No one else knows?

HAROLD
Naturally, my doctor knows. And the odd divine, tawny attendant. Actually, I don't care who knows I have AIDS, I just don't want anyone to know I'm gay.
[*He turns toward the front door.*]

MICHAEL
Where're you going?!

HAROLD
Home to that heavenly creature.

MICHAEL
Wait a minute.

HAROLD
[*Turns back*]
Why?

MICHAEL
[*Heatedly serious*]
Oh, Harold, you can't be that glib about mortality!

HAROLD
[*Eyeball to eyeball*]
I can.
[*A pause. They continue to look at each other directly...*]

MICHAEL
[*Heartfelt, quietly*]
I'll be there for you, you know that.

HAROLD
[*Seriously*]
It never crossed my mind that you wouldn't be.
[*A beat*]
That is, if you don't perish in a private plane crash on your next
junket to the Cote D'Azur.
[*After a moment, with meaning*]
I know you'll do whatever I want. Whatever it takes—fight City
Hall, face the dawn with arms linked, ride a *float* even.

MICHAEL
[*Without rancor*]
Harold, I'm serious.

HAROLD
I know you are, and that's why I can't be.

MICHAEL
[*After a moment*]
We'll get through this together.
[HAROLD *is both touched and made somewhat anxious by the
genuine declaration of love for him.*]

HAROLD
[*Turns to leave*]
I really do have to go now, and I'm not just trying to get out of
here—although I'm trying like hell to get out of here.
[*Old brand of wryness*]
I don't want blondie to break the Lalique samovar.
[*Goes, stops, turns, says genuinely*]
I had such spilkus I just couldn't *not* not tell you any longer. I
know that's a triple negative, but fuck it. When I heard you speak
at the memorial this afternoon, I knew I had to come clean.

HAROLD

I liked what you said about Larry. I hope you'll say a few words about me...

MICHAEL

Harold.

HAROLD

Something like "He was a smart-ass with heart. A Scorpio with vulnerability."

[*MICHAEL nods, refusing to give in to the moment...*]

MICHAEL

I'll think of something.

[*Then, sincerely*]

I do wish you would have told me earlier.

HAROLD

I didn't want anybody there!

MICHAEL

[*Incredulously*]

You didn't want *me* there?! *Me*, of all people?!

HAROLD

Yes, you of all people!

MICHAEL

How can you say a thing like that about me?!

HAROLD

Now you sound like my mother!

MICHAEL

[*Sardonically*]

By the way, tell me, is your mother still dead?

HAROLD

[*Half incensed, half amused*]

She is presently deceased, yes. But when I'm around you, I'm not so sure!

[*Hating what he's about to say*]

You know, nobody, *nobody* can get to me the way you and my mother can!

[*Corrects himself*]

Could!

[*Quickly*]
Can!
[*Tries again*]
Could...and can!

MICHAEL
Calm down.

HAROLD
Oh, eat shit and die!

MICHAEL
You have every right to be angry.

HAROLD
You know, I think I liked you better when you were drunk!

MICHAEL
You know what? I liked *you* better when I was drunk too!

HAROLD
[*Quickly, with "dignity"*]
I also think with whatever time I have left, I oughtta start hanging out with a better class of losers!

MICHAEL
[*Matching him*]
Well, you can start tonight in your own bed!

HAROLD
[*Matching him*]
At least, there's somebody *in my bed tonight*!

MICHAEL
[*"Grandly"*]
I hate you when you get like this.

HAROLD
[*"Philosophically"*]
Well, you *are* what you *hate*.

MICHAEL
[*Wearily*]
Oh, Harold, let's *not*!

HAROLD
[*Fiercely vulgar*]
No, goddamn it, *let's*!

MICHAEL
[*Evenly*]
We're too old for this game!!

HAROLD
[*Facetiously*]
Too analyzed, too grown up, too mature?!

MICHAEL
Yes! And too *old*!

HAROLD
I'm the one who's analyzed, grown up, and mature! *You're* just old!
You peaked at eighteen, and it's been downhill ever since. And you
are now fifty-nine and counting!

MICHAEL
Thank you and fuck you!!
    [*MICHAEL quickly picks up HAROLD's rain cape and umbrella and
    tosses them to him.*]

MICHAEL
GETOUTTAHERE!

HAROLD
[*Exiting apartment*]
CALLYATOMORROW!!!
    [*MICHAEL slams the front door. After a moment, MICHAEL turns, slow-
    ly goes to open the bar. He stands, looking at all the colored bottles and
    sparkling glasses. As MICHAEL stands staring at the tempting dis-
    play...(will he or won't he?)...slowly, all lights fade to black.*]

E N D   O F   A C T   2

E N D   O F   P L A Y

About Mart Crowley

Mart Crowley was born in Vicksburg, Mississippi, and educated at the Catholic University of America in Washington, D.C. His plays include *The Boys in the Band* (New York, 1968; London, 1969); *Remote Asylum* (Los Angeles, 1970); A Breeze From the Gulf (New York, 1973; London, 1991); *Avec Schmaltz* (Williamstown, Massachussetts Theatre Festival, 1984); *For Reasons That Remain Unclear* (Olney, Maryland, 1993); and *The Men From the Boys* (San Francisco, 2002; Los Angeles, 2003). Crowley also adapted and produced the film version of *The Boys in the Band* and produced the long-running television series *Hart to Hart*. In addition, he edited and completed Kay Thompson's children's book *Eloise Takes a Bath* (Simon & Schuster, 2002).

About Donald Spoto

Donald Spoto earned his Ph.D. from Fordham University. He has published 19 books, including *The Kindness of Strangers: The Life of Tennessee Williams*; *Laurence Olivier: A Biography*; and *The Dark Side of Genius: The Life of Alfred Hitchcock*.